Bittersweet

INDIGO RIVER
PUBLISHING

Bittersweet

KRISTEN CATHEY

Indigo River Publishing

Indigo River Publishing
3 West Garden Street Ste. 352 M
Pensacola, FL 32502
www.indigoriverpublishing.com

Book Design: mycustombookcover.com

Editor: Earl Tillinghast, Regina Cornell

Ordering Information: Quantity sales: Special discounts are available on quantity purchases by corporations, associations, and others. For details, contact the publisher at the address above.

Orders by U.S. trade bookstores and wholesalers: Please contact the publisher at the address above.

Printed in the United States of America

Library of Congress Control Number: 2018940012

ISBN: 978-1-948080-23-1

First Edition

With Indigo River Publishing, you can always expect great books, strong voices, and meaningful messages. Most importantly, you'll always find … words worth reading.

Dedication

To my family: I dedicate this book to you as there is nothing more important. This book was inspired and created because of you.

To my husband: I will never be able to describe how thankful I am to have you by my side. From the age of nineteen 'til now, God gave us thirteen beautiful years to tackle together. I thank you for believing in me and my dreams. The journey God created for us has been the best adventure, with many unexpected turns, and I cannot wait for the next chapter in our lives.

To my son: You are the hope for the future. You have impacted and changed my life in so many ways, and that has created a bond that I will never let go. You are the reason to fight for another day. I can only humble myself with the responsibility that Jesus gave me to raise you. Though I make mistakes and I don't always deserve to raise you, I hope you can see my love for you will always be here. I hope I taught you how much Jesus loves you, and if you are willing to work, you can achieve anything; plus, I will be by your side cheering you on every step of the way.

Last but not least, I dedicate this book to God, who knows my sins and my heart. Jesus, you are my God and I humble myself to you. I pray my path leads to you and straightens my sins of the past and my hopes for the future. You are my strength at my weakest point, and everything I have is your blessing.

I dedicate this book to my strength, love, and passion. To God, Bobby, and Logan: thank you for your love, kindness, and support.

Prologue

Casey, though struggling and tired, finally reaches the top of the cliff. She turns her head, and ten feet in front of her is a mountain lion standing on top of a boulder, staring her down. She stumbles backward, caught off guard by the presence of the animal, and falls to the ground. Her head hangs over the cliff causing her neck and jaw muscles to cramp up, sending shocks of pain down her back. Taking her eyes off the big cat for just a second, she looks over the edge of the cliff, knowing she could fall off. Turning back to the animal, she looks into its beautiful blue marble eyes. He must be deciding how to attack me, she thinks. I'm so vulnerable and my only option is not to fall off the edge. Steadying her composure, she takes a deep breath and narrows her eyes to look as mean and fearless as she can.

He knows he has her right where he wants her. With an evil smirk and a twinkle in his eyes, the lion knows his dinner is right in front of him. She watches the mountain lion slightly bend its knees as it digs into the boulder, and then it quickly jumps down to the same level as her. He slightly opens his mouth, showing his sharp teeth that he wants to dig into her, gives a loud hissing sound, and licks his lips. Casey knows she must survive; she has to protect herself from the pain that is about to be inflicted upon her. She must think fast on what to do next; he is coming for her. Unable to move from the fear and shock that has taken over her body, she watches the lion ready to pounce. Suddenly Komodo reaches the top of the cliff and jumps right between them. Everything is happening so fast she cannot wrap her head around it…

Chapter 1

Casey is doing her usual grocery shopping for the day with her six-year-old son, Lincoln, who is running to the Christmas trees on display, flaunting with blinking red and green lights. He loves the all too familiar traditional holiday scene, with charming caroling music in the background. It is early November, and she finds it amazing that the Christmas season is in full swing in all the grocery and department stores. Wrapping paper is displayed creatively on the shelves in the aisle, and all the new toys are out for the season, begging to be purchased to make some children's dreams come true. Her presents are already purchased for this year, and she is deciding how to finish decorating their house. This Christmas is very exciting for Casey's family because it's the first one in their new home. They already have the stockings hung up and the Christmas tree displayed decoratively with ornaments and lights that twinkle at night. All that is left is to string the rest of the lights, wrap the presents, and place them under the tree. Lincoln is going to have a lot of fun this year because he can really tear open the presents and he understands who Saint Nicolaus and Jesus are. Embracing the spirit of Christmas, his imagination can run wild. After all, this is what the holidays are all about: the joy of the child believing in something more than what is around him. The innocence of a child is truly priceless.

As he jumps up and down, giggling his way down the aisle, Casey tries to get Linc back to the shopping cart so they can head over to the food aisles to pick up taco ingredients for dinner, which is her husband's favorite. Just as she catches up to her son, the store lights flicker on and off, she hears gasps from nearby people, and she freezes. "Linc," she calls, with a worried voice. He stops and then dashes back to his mother.

The next thing they hear is a big, explosive noise bursting throughout the store, making her look up to see lights from the ceiling shatter. Glass is flying down like shooting stars heading right at them, like the electricity went into overdrive and could not handle the current rushing through the wires, causing them to burst. Trying to shield Lincoln from any harm, she drops her body over him protectively, breathing deeply to calm herself, yet ready for pain should glass penetrate her skin. Other parents and children are yelling and screaming all around them. Linc is quiet, and she feels the heat from both of their breaths in this enclosed space. The explosive noise takes only a few seconds. With such a quick burst of danger, it's over as fast as it came. Holding her breath, she thinks, *1, 2, 3...* This always helps Casey bring her body under control, ready to face whatever high-pressure issue she is dealing with. Finally, they look up and see that the whole store is dark and silent.

"Are you OK? Tell Mommy you are OK," she says, checking her son for glass, first his dirty blonde hair, then his arms. Next, she shakes off his T-shirt and pants to make sure no glass stuck to his clothes. Lastly, his mother cups his face with both of her hands on each side of his rosy red cheeks to see if there are any scratches on it. Feeling better knowing he is not bleeding, she sees his big brown eyes look at her with irritation while he tries to pull his head away. He gives her the all too knowing look, and she thinks if anything ever happened to him, she would blame herself. This is her job as a mom: to make sure her child is safe.

"Mommy, I'm fine! What is going on anyways? Wow, it is really dark in here!" he says.

"Give me your hand now, son." Grabbing it, she ignores his questions, not sure what to say. *Maybe the electricity will turn back on soon,* she thinks. Standing up, she looks around, now that her eyes have adjusted to the dark, and sees people picking glass out of their hair and others looking at their cuts, deciding how to deal with their injuries. Many groups are looking around, just as confused as she is. With her adrenaline in high gear, she is ready to get out of here and quickly shakes the glass off her clothes.

Leaving their shopping cart behind, they walk toward the door, noticing the cashiers are not ringing anything up. People are starting to complain and yell about what just happened. Some employees are directing injured people together into a group, while others are running to them with first aid products. Lastly, she sees employees directing most of the people to the doors and out of the store. The backup generator has not turned on, and there is nothing but darkness. An eerie feeling races through her body, making the hair on her neck stand on end. She squeezes Linc's hand tightly to make sure he is still with her as her mind tells her to get out as fast as she can.

Walking fast toward the doors, where the only light is coming into the building, she keeps her head straight, trying not to be noticed or show she is panicking. Her heart is racing a mile a minute, and it takes everything in her not to run outside. She stops walking, closes her eyes to calm down, and counts under her breath, "1, 2, 3…" Then, more relaxed, she opens her eyes and continues to walk.

"Come on, Linc, let's go home. We will come back tomorrow when the lights are on." Before they go outside, she bends over to help him put his coat on and zips it up; then she takes care of her own.

"But we did not get any food, Mommy," he says.

"I know, son. We will have to make a different meal for Daddy when we get home. Come on, please hurry."

Stepping out of the store with a group of people, they find the winter air is cold and crisp, which makes Casey's nose sting. It is refreshing after being in the dark, musty building, and she squints her eyes until they adjust to the bright sun, allowing her to focus on walking to the truck. There is a thin blanket of melting snow reflecting crystal rays up at their faces, intensifying the brightness. Linc splashes the slushy snow with his boots while she tugs on his arm to keep him moving toward the truck.

"Look, Mommy, at my tracks in the snow," he says, while pressing his feet in the slush, then pointing at his creation.

"I see your footprints, son," she says, not looking behind her, still tugging on his arm. They walk down to the truck where they left Komodo, their dog, and she puts Linc in his seat and then turns the key, but the truck will not start. She tries again and again, but it refuses to turn over. Finally, out of frustration, she pulls out her cell phone to call Devon for help. Her husband always comes to save the day; this is one of the things that she loves about him. He's always there to get her out of trouble, whether she locks the truck with her keys in the ignition or it breaks down. He always finds a way to take care of her. Looking at her phone, which is black with no screen images, she's confused. The power button will not work, yet it was working before they went into the store. *What is going on here?* This is really making her nervous. *How come my truck will not work? I have never had a problem starting it before and have never had an issue with my cell phone. None of this makes sense. Too many problems are happening at once. Now what am I going to do? What would my husband do?*

The rearview mirror reflects her son petting his best friend and partner in crime: big, white, fluffy Komodo. He and the dog will chase each other and play all day. Anytime Linc is up to something his dog is standing right next to him. Casey smiles at the thought. Since Lincoln is an only child, they wanted to make sure he had a buddy at home.

Their other dog, a purebred pit bull, is named Baby Girl. She is older, about ten, and not too excited about playing; mostly she wants to sleep. Her coat is white with black spots that have brindle highlights that shine in the light. She has one black spot around her left eye, while her right eye is white. She gets active if she feels the need to protect them, but other than that, Baby Girl prefers to lie on the couch all day. This is what inspired Casey to get a new puppy for her son. Komodo and Linc connected from the start, which made her excited to see them get along so well. It is such an endearing sight to see one of those classic companionships that people see or read about. Linc truly has a loyal companion by his side; and his dog is not just loyal to her son either, he is loyal to the whole family.

Looking around the parking lot, nobody can get their car to start. Many people are trying unsuccessfully, while others are looking under the hoods of the cars trying to figure out why, but nothing is changing. Her mind starts to race in a million ways. *Can it be? Can this really be happening?* Running wild, her imagination can get the best of her. She can get lost in her own thoughts all day long, thinking of the most extreme in any situation. Her mind takes over, and she thinks about movies where the enemy takes down the power grid and once the people start running out of food they get desperate and kill each other.

No, stop it! This is just a coincidence. Casey's mind is putting her into panic mode and running a mile a minute. *I must keep cool so I can make good decisions to keep my son safe. I need to keep it together for him; and right now there is no electricity, cars will not start, and my phone doesn't work. It's the middle of winter with snow on the ground, and I have a six-year-old and his dog to take care of. This is not my ideal situation. The only thing that I can do is get home.*

"Are we going, Mom?" Linc asks, killing her train of thought.

What else is there to do? We cannot sit here in our truck all day. I must get across town to our house, and I need to stay calm. This is going to be a long walk with a six-year-old, but what choice do I have? I just do not trust people enough to ask for help.

Casey has always been the kind of person who keeps more to herself. She has friends but just a few close ones, and she is not interested in letting a lot of people into her life. With her heightened sense of paranoia, she worries that others may hurt her family. There are so many stories in the news of women being attacked for no reason, which make her feel vulnerable when she is by herself or with her son. It is not like she is strong or has ever had to defend herself. She wouldn't know where to begin if somebody attacked her. Therefore, she brings her sixty-pound Great Pyrenees everywhere she goes. Only eight months old, he has a strong bark and is very aware of his surroundings. Other people always think twice about coming too close, which makes her feel safe. Even though he has always been a gentle giant, she learned from research that he is designed to protect his herd, and their family is his herd.

"Yes, son, we are walking home."

"Walking home—oh man."

Looking in the review mirror again, she sees Linc glaring at her. His big brown eyes are narrowed and piercing. He crosses his arms in protest, pulling them up to his small chest to show strength before he says, "I do not want to walk. That is boring. Walking is boring!"

Intentionally ignoring him so they do not start a confrontation, she needs him to listen right now to get this process going. Opening the console of her truck, she pulls out a .22-caliber handgun that is small enough to stuff in her pocket, which her husband insists she carry around. He taught her to shoot and to use a bow; she has hunted a couple of times and set up a few traps in the woods. Devon felt this information was important, and she always tried to learn whatever he showed her because she loves him and enjoys his company. They would go into the woods together, and he would teach her everything he knew about hunting and survival. She tried to listen and pay attention, but really, she just enjoyed hiking through the hills and camping near the lakes, which is always a nice way to get away from all the city noise.

Calming her nerves, she closes her eyes, takes a deep breath, *1, 2, 3...* and then says a little prayer quietly: "Please, Jesus, keep us safe and keep my husband safe, too."

Getting out of the truck, she opens Linc's door to let him out. Komodo follows behind, and she grabs the leash hanging from his collar. With one hand holding her son and her other hand holding their dog's leash, they start the journey through town.

<h1 style="text-align:center">Chapter 2</h1>

I sure hope my husband is at home, she thinks, as they stomp through the slushy snow on their way down the sidewalk, though Casey knows in her heart he is not. He is at work right now, nowhere near their house, and if he were closer she would walk to him, but unfortunately he is across the other side of town. *I can do this; we can walk to our house. Be strong is what my husband would expect from me. The safety of our child comes first. He is in my hands, and I must make good decisions every step of the way.*

It is sometime before noon, and the sun is rising in the sky, which feels good on her face with the rays absorbing into her skin. The air is cold, but they have their heavy coats and gloves on to keep warm. South Dakota can have bitter winters that can nip anybody if they are out too long; plus, the wind whips around making it feel colder. In this kind of weather, their Pyrenees is fine, with his two thick layers of fur, and he comes alive when it is cold outside. But she worries about her son getting too cold; therefore, they need to get home before the sun goes down. *At least at home we have blankets to help keep us warm. Better yet, maybe the electricity did not go out and we can have some heat.*

As they make their way down the blocks she sees people standing outside of their houses, talking to their neighbors about what just happened. One group is talking about how they have no electricity and are worried about the food in the refrigerator, and another group is saying their cell phones are not working. Seeing so many people walking, she realizes that the grocery store is not the only place having this issue, which makes her pick up the pace. Linc's little legs can't keep up, and she starts to drag him as her attention and thoughts are on Devon. *I am sure he couldn't get his car working either and is just as confused about what is going on. He is probably thinking we are safe at the house or is at least hoping so.*

"Mommy, we need to slow down. I told you my legs are tired," Linc states in his know-it-all voice.

"We have to keep walking to get home," she says, but still slows down so he can catch up. Several blocks later they make it downtown to the main shopping district in Rapid City, a little historical area with cobbled sidewalks of brick matching the older buildings that have been turned into shops and restaurants. People love to come here and hang out, enjoying the many activities for families that get the community together. Since Casey is not a big social person, she does not come down here much or keep up on what is going on. All she knows is: they need to go through this area on Main Street to make it to their subdivision that's on the other side.

A lot of people are standing outside looking around, and as she gets closer she can hear them talking to each other about how the stores lost power and their vehicles wouldn't start. They pass by a young couple who seem nervous, talking fast about their problems with their cell phones. *The whole town must be out of power.*

She decides that it would be faster to go straight through the alleys behind the buildings that connect to the other side. People are bunching up on the sidewalk, and she does not want to drag her son through the crowd and take a chance on losing him.

Stepping into the alley, she notices it is quieter between the buildings, and darker as they block out the sunlight. She feels a few degrees colder, causing her to shiver. With just a couple of people hanging around, Casey watches a group of guys smirking wickedly at them as they pass by, whispering to each other and staring like they know some secret, making her hair stand on end. *Maybe we should have gone through the crowd.* She grabs Linc's hand tighter, pulling him closer. Showing his teeth, their dog narrows his eyes and gives a nasty growl, telling the guys to stay back. They stop smiling at once and look away. *Good boy, Komodo,* she thinks, while looking over her shoulder to make sure they are not following; then she picks up the pace to get out of there.

As they pass by the openings between the buildings where the streets intersect, she sees the crowd is much bigger than before. There must be a thousand people or more just standing around. *Are we the only ones trying to get somewhere? Don't they want to get home before the sun goes down, or do they think, if they wait, everything will just work again?*

Looking down the road before crossing the street into the next alley, Casey observes the people on Main Street clearing the area. Then she hears a loud, roaring noise, sounding like a large truck. Between the buildings there is an opening, and she can see a military tank, camouflaged with a green camo pattern and with a big gun on the top, moving slowly as it reaches the spot to set up. Behind the tank are four yellow school buses, all with bars in the windows and soldiers inside. After the tank stops a man steps out on top of the military vehicle, looking down at the crowd.

He puts a large megaphone to his mouth, so they can all hear what he has to say: "Everybody, please." He pauses, looking at the crowd until they give him their attention. "Please stay calm and wait right here; we will take you to a safe place. The electricity has gone down throughout the whole town, and we have people working on the grid to fix it. In the meantime, we are here to help, and we have a building where we can take you to stay warm until this issue is resolved. One of the main backup generators we have is working, so please line up in front of the buses, and we can get everybody to where it is safe and warm."

He seems helpful, speaking in clear English. Though of average height for a man, he looks bigger standing on the tank and more authoritative with his military uniform. With a frozen face and stern eyes that look like daggers, Casey assumes he must be important to the military because everybody is listening to him.

The crowd calmly lines up to each of the buses as the doors open to let them in. The soldiers step out in front of the vehicles, looking at the crowd. Casey thinks they will have to do a couple of trips before they can get everybody to their safe place. *This problem with the grid could take a long time to fix. It could be days, even weeks before the electricity is back on. Do I trust this man? Maybe they are the National Guard, but how did they get here so fast and so well organized? It's like they knew this was going to happen, yet the citizens had no idea what is going on. Why do I keep questioning their motives? Man, I must be paranoid.*

There are at least a hundred uniformed soldiers lined up in their designated spots, all organized and ready to go. Some are standing still on guard, and others are walking around talking to the citizens. She can see they have already been given their orders and are following their commander to the T. Every one of them has a gun and is using it to direct the people.

Their guns are a lot bigger than mine, she thinks, contemplating this issue while hiding behind a building in the alley as more and more people continue to line up. She sees an older woman and some small children step into the bus as the guy on the megaphone continues directing the lines. *Why would the army need these guns? Nobody is hostile here, and if they are American, they should just be helping, not protecting themselves. Plus, how are the buses running but not the citizens' cars, and why are there bars on the bus windows? None of this makes any sense, and not understanding is making me fearful to leave our hiding spot.* Noticing a man pushing through the crowd away from the buses and in their direction, she hears him yell, "Run, everybody, run!"

Shoving people out of his way, he sprints away from the soldiers and the crowd, who look confused as they open a path way for him. Then Casey looks past him to see a soldier point his gun, aim, and shoot a bullet that zips through the crowd at full force right into his back! The bullet flies through him and exits out of his chest, passing by the alley. They watch blood spit through the air while he falls to the ground. Thud—his knees bang the pavement as he tilts his head up in their direction for just a second, making her think he is looking at her, before his body fully collapses to the ground. Time holds still like the shooting happened in slow motion. She can hear the thump…thump of her own blood rushing through her veins as the crowd watches this man fall to his death.

Then, at the speed of light, her brain comes back to the reality from screams of the people. Like chickens with their heads cut off, they begin to run in all directions, trying to get away from the soldiers. Mass chaos begins as people flee for safety. Some drop to the ground and get trampled while others try to jump over them. Soldiers line up in front of the buses and the tank, shooting at everybody like it is open season of pheasant hunting. They shoot and then step forward in complete unison, hitting people who are running and who are lying on the ground, with no mercy for the men, women, or even children—they are killing everybody! *This is completely crazy,* Casey thinks, and starts to panic as she hears gunshots in all directions, sounding like firecrackers as they pop off. She knows now why the soldiers are lined up: so the vehicles protect their backs as they take slow, steady steps forward, advancing toward the crowd, killing as they go, while others shove victims into the buses to trap them inside. This has just turned into a full-fledged massacre of the people!

Casey shoves Linc around the other side of the building, against the wall, hiding him from the chaos, while slamming her own back forcefully as well. Almost knocking the wind out of herself, wanting to shield them both from the bullets, she makes eye contact with her son, then puts her finger to her lips to indicate that he should be quiet. His eyes are huge with fear, and he grabs her hand as hard as he can with his little muscles, but stays very quiet. Then she looks down at Komodo, pointing her finger to the ground, and he lays low on all four paws, putting out a quiet growl at the same time, with his hair standing up in anticipation. Since she has had this dog she spent time training him to listen. Using different noises and hand signals, he knows exactly what she wants, which makes her grateful; if he barks, they are going to be in trouble.

Putting her hand in her pocket, she pulls out her gun and cocks it so it is ready to be used, now wishing it were bigger. *What is my little .22 going to do against their big whatever type of gun they have? Maybe it is a rifle or an automatic assault rifle, but really, I have no idea. I just know it is bigger and stronger than mine and wish I had paid more attention to my husband; he would know what guns the soldiers have and how far they can accurately shoot. This information would be good to know right about now.*

Closing her eyes, she takes a deep breath and counts 1, 2, 3... then opens her eyes again. Looking around the corner of the building, she sees people are still being shot and hears the piercing screams from the crowd as they push and trample through to protect themselves from the soldiers. There is so much blood everywhere and so much going on at once! She needs to get out of here fast! *What would my husband do?* her brain screams. Casey looks across the alley and sees a big commercial dumpster. *If I run across the street to the other alley, I have a high chance of being shot, and I do not have the gun power that can shoot back with the same accuracy. Plus, I do not even know if I have good enough aim to hit my target. This is way too much risk on my son's life. No, not a good option.*

Scooting Linc over to the dumpster, she opens the lid and puts her gun back in her pocket, picks up her son, and places him inside. Komodo leaps up with his front paws, catching the edge of the dumpster and gripping it with his claws. Casey reaches down underneath his back paws with her hands and shoves him up as he jumps inside. Finally, she climbs in last and shuts the lid. The smell is disgusting as it fills her nostrils with a repulsive, rotting, spoiled scent. She uses all the energy that she has not to throw up everywhere. The garbage is squishy as she tries to steady herself in this nasty mess underneath. Komodo moves behind her, and she grabs Linc harshly, putting him between them, and pulls his coat up to his nose in an attempt to keep the smell away from him. Linc closes his eyes as he tries to keep the stench from entering his body while holding on to his coat for dear life. Lastly, Casey steadies herself and grabs her gun, pointing it at the lid.

"This is serious; we have to be very quiet and still." Linc is scared, frozen in silence from the intensity of his mom's voice.

It seems like they have sat in this nasty dumpster for a long time, with her gun in the air, ready to shoot the first person who opens the lid. Her adrenaline is in overdrive, and she can hear her heart trying to beat out of her chest, while her arms shake from holding the gun in a stretched-out position. Linc leans on his dog, trying to keep warm. Komodo is still on all four paws, ready to jump up to protect his family. Although she never trained him to protect them, he does it by nature and has shown he wants to keep them safe by the way he sleeps in front of their bed-room doors at night, sits in front of the bathroom when somebody is in it, or keeps an eye on everything in the back yard. This makes her feel like she is not the only one trying to keep her son safe. His presence gives her a small amount of confidence that if somebody tries to hurt them, her dog will protect them or give them a chance to run away.

Listening to the firework sounds of the gunshots that never seem to stop, once again her mind drifts back to her husband. *Is he safe? Maybe he is heading home right now and nothing bad has happened to him or he found a way to make a car work.* Suddenly the garbage lid swings wide open, with her finger on the trigger, ready to pull, and her head screams, *No! Do not shoot! This face I know!* Then she realizes it is Jamie from school. She was about to shoot her good friend in the face, so ready to react to the chaos of the day. *What are the chances that I would see someone familiar in this madness?* Casey lowers her gun so Jamie knows that she is safe, making her smile in relief, realizing it is someone she knows, and she immediately hops into the dumpster. Shutting the lid behind her, she looks at her school mate and tries to control her breathing. Jamie's face is smeared with blood and dirt, and Casey thinks that she must have been running hard.

Originally meeting in high school, they had most of the same classes together. Though Casey was always quiet, Jamie was not. She was pop-ular; all the guys wanted her attention, and though it was obvious, she acted like she didn't notice. She was voted the prettiest girl and became the prom queen at their dance, but she was truly friends with everybody. The first time Casey met her, she had walked into their ninth-grade math class and pulled her thick blonde hair out of a ponytail, which allowed it to fall down lightly onto her shoulders. All the guys in the room were staring, but she acted like she didn't notice. Instead, she sat next to the shy girl in the back. They looked at each other, and she said, "Hey, I'm Jamie. Can I hide back here with you? Math is pretty tough for me."

Surprised at her comments, the shy girl replied, "Sure. My name is Casey." Since that time they have been good friends, sitting together at lunch or hanging out after school. Even though their lives went in different directions as they got older, both managed to stay in touch throughout the years.

In relief, Jamie lunges across the garbage and hugs her friend for a split second, then pulls away. "Thank God," she whispers, and they both turn to stare at the closed lid again. Komodo gives a low growl, unsure if he should trust her. His nose is twitching, trying to smell her from across the dumpster. Casey looks at him with a glare in her eyes, and he submits at once; then she looks up at the dumpster lid again. Now all of them stare, quietly waiting, for they knew they cannot speak; it is just too dangerous. Casey hopes the soldiers did not see Jamie get into the dumpster; she does not want their cover to be blown. *What would we do if they found us? Are we just waiting for a soldier to open the lid and shoot us or take us away? At least we have a small advantage: my gun can shoot close range, and any face I see I will shoot.*

After a few minutes of sitting in the dumpster as quietly as they can, the sounds of people running and screaming fill the alley, echoing in their ears! The screams bounce off the metal walls, vibrating throughout their bodies. Casey believes they must be right outside. She leans back against her son, believing this to be the time she will have to use her gun. She braces herself for the impact of what is about to happen. *Here we go!* The sounds of rifle shots are close enough to take over the sounds of the screams. Out of the corner of her eye, she sees Linc pushing his head into his dog for comfort, trying to hide from the horror. Locking herself into position, ready for the worst, the moment of truth, Casey is ready to die for her son and kill anyone who tries to hurt him. Her gun is cocked, with a finger on the trigger waiting to squeeze.

Taking a deep breath, she counts in her head, *1, 2, 3...,* exhales, takes another deep breath, and waits. They try to be as silent and still as possible, like statues slowly sinking in the trash. Thud! The sound cuts the air like a knife and Casey shudders; then they hear nothing but silence. The screams just fell to the ground; no more voices and no more struggles to live. It is so quiet a pin could drop and they would be able to hear it. After a few seconds of silence they hear strong footsteps walking closer to the dumpster. *There has to be at least two people walking, if not more,* she guesses. They are not screaming or running. Their footsteps sound slow and in control. They have to be the shooters, not scared of their lives because they are the ones taking others. *I hate them! If I were stronger, had more protection, I would show them what I could do!*

She swears everybody can hear her heart racing in her chest, trying to jump out with this throbbing feeling; she thinks it may burst. Looking around quickly, Casey sees Jamie's eyes are closed and assumes she is praying. Immediately her attention returns to the lid, still in position to shoot whoever opens it. With her little gun, their only chance is to surprise the soldier and get him right in the face. These seconds seem like forever, with the anticipation of death slowly smiling in their faces. *One wrong move, one crunch of the garbage, and the soldiers will have us.* Then they hear the footsteps moving. *Are they walking away?* Once Casey cannot hear them anymore she lets out a sigh of relief and thanks God they did not investigate the dumpster, knowing that it was a close call. After holding the gun so tightly her knuckles turned white, she finally relaxes and shakes her hand, feeling the tingling rush of blood back to her fingers.

It feels like forever before they hear no more gunshots, scary footsteps, or screaming. The silence finally sets in and makes the ringing sound in her ears turn up. *Is this because of the guns shots echoing earlier, or is my hearing on high alert?* Jamie stares at Casey. *She must be wondering what I am thinking. She looks like she is ready to see what is going on outside.* Linc adjusts his body so he can stretch out his legs. *How long have we been in this nasty trash?* She wants to make sure that nobody is around them before they check out what's going on. Finally, Jamie nods her head and opens the lid very softly, trying not to disturb the eerie silence. Casey pokes her head over the ledge of the dumpster and looks down the alley in both directions. After seeing nothing she is ready to venture out. Looking at Linc, who is still leaning on Komodo, she whispers, "Hey, I am going to step out for a second. You stay here. I will be right back." He nods his head to show he understands, though she can see he is scared.

She helps Jamie push the lid fully open and lifts her legs over the edge of the dumpster, placing her feet on the pavement. Her Pyrenees pokes his head out of their hiding place with his ears standing up, trying to hear everything while looking around to see if it safe. Once he is content he points his nose to the sky to smell the fresh air, which is inviting after sitting in the horrible dumpster. At the same time, she starts to slowly close the lid, making him lower his head and causing her dog to whimper, not wanting to be left behind.

Raising her gun, ready to shoot at anybody who pops out, her flight-or-fight instincts are in full gear. She turns away from the dumpster to see the violent scene of what they heard earlier. Absorbing this chaos, she sees a girl lying on her stomach with blood pooled all around her, which clearly shows she was running for her life. There are a couple of bullet wounds in her back. Her face is lying on its side against the pavement, mouth wide open in a silent scream and eyes frozen in fear. This girl had to be only eighteen. Sadness sweeps over Casey as she stares at the girl's thick, dark hair tangled with blood all over her stained black-and-white checker-patterned coat. She shudders, trying to shake away the truth of what happened here. *What a horror! She was too young to die, with so much life to live that is now all gone.* She bends down next to this young girl, and with shaking fingers she closes the girl's eyes to help put her to peace. Struggling to hold it together and trying not to cry, Casey turns her head away and pukes all over the pavement, unable to control her stomach anymore. Wiping her mouth, she then looks back at the girl, thinking, *I did not know her name, family, anything.* Wobbling as she stands up, she closes her eyes, trying to shove the sorrow aside, turns her back to this pain, takes a breath, and moves on.

Stepping over the dead girl's body, she heads over to the corner of the building where they originally started and listens for a few seconds, but hears nothing. No shooting, vehicles, nothing, just an eerie silence. The stillness is just as scary as the noise from the shooting and screaming. Casey closes her eyes and counts 1, 2, 3…, breathes, and then opens her eyes. She peeks around the corner of the building and sees nothing but dead bodies everywhere, like a bloody graveyard. Horrified, she squeezes her eyes shut again, focusing on her breathing, before she forces them open and sees that the soldiers, tanks, and buses are gone. Looking at the ground, she is shocked to see so many dead people—too many—who are victims of this massacre. These people had no chance or warning. A few hours ago they were all enjoying life, shopping and eating, unaware of their fate. *Who could do such a horrible act of violence? This cannot be our government who would do this to their own people, not the people we elected into office to represent us. They wouldn't do such a hate crime. This must be terrorists; who else would hunt us down like animals, sheep for the slaughter?*

Snow soaks up the blood that blankets the ground, making the people look cold, their bodies stiff and lifeless, fear showing in their eyes. *So many souls lost today for no reason.* Like a knife stabbing her in the lungs, she gasps for air while taking in this carnage. *This could have been us if I had chosen to walk through the crowd.* They would have had no chance either, which torments her mind as the disturbing slaughter is right in front of her face. She pulls back around the building into the alley, pushing herself against the wall as fast as she can, wanting to run away from the blood bath that lies before her. Closing her eyes, she bangs her head against the wall, trying to push those fearful dead faces out of her mind.

Muttering quietly, she prays: "Thank you, Jesus, for protecting us. Please keep our family alive." She keeps her eyes closed, trying to control her breathing, counts again, 1, 2, 3… and then opens them slowly with her body in control. Her instinct kicks in again, and she knows what she needs to do. *We must keep moving and get out of here as fast as we can.* Freezing her emotions, she steps over the dead girl in the alley and goes back to the dumpster.

"Come on, Linc. We have to get out of here now," she says after she opens the lid and grabs his arms. Komodo jumps out of the dumpster by himself, ready to escape from the captivity of the nasty trash. Jamie follows next, lifting herself out, and then stares at the girl on the ground in front of them. "Jamie, they are gone, and we have to get out of here. Where are you going?" Choosing not to say anything about the blood bath on Main Street since she cannot do anything to help, she thinks, *They deserve better, someone to find their IDs, give them a proper burial, and tell their stories, but they will be left in the streets, ignored.* This is all too overwhelming for Casey, and a sadness flows through her. Again, she pushes the pain down into her gut to control her tears for her son. *I will harden my face and cry later by myself, when we are safe and when I have time to deal with my emotions, but until then I need to find my inner strength and put on the best show. I'll look cool and in control, the way the soldiers did, and find some paper somewhere to write down what has happened here. Their story will not go untold,* she thinks, justifying in her mind why she is walking away from this horror. Holding Linc in her arms with his legs wrapped around her waist, she pushes his head into her shoulder to hide him from the body in the alley.

Still staring at the dead girl, Jamie is lost in thoughts about what happened earlier. Casey sees the panic in her crystal-blue eyes. "I have no idea. Can I come with you?" With the aftermath of blood and dirt on her face Casey knows something traumatic has happened to her, but this is not the time to talk about it. She does not want Linc to hear anything about this rampage of hate.

"I don't know what we are doing next, except to try to get to the house. But you can come with us if you want. I'm hoping my husband is there. He will know what to do."

Jamie nods her head and her lips tremble. "Lead the way," she says, her eyes still staring at the dead girl. Finally, she forces herself to turn away from the victim and comes back to reality.

Chapter 3

Scurrying as fast as they can, crossing the intersection into the next alley, Casey tries to block her son from the bodies, attempting to keep the images out his head, knowing he has had enough for the day. This is the quietest she has ever seen him. He is normally so full of life, always contradicting everything because in his mind he knows best. But today she sees a very tired, worried child. His perfect schedule of life has been destroyed.

Quietly creeping through downtown and neighborhoods, they finally make it to their block. Watching a cluster of neighbors, Casey can tell they are talking about the problems, but they are so lucky to be stuck at their houses, to not have dead faces flashing through their minds, and, most of all, to not be victims on Main Street. *If we had only been here when all these problems occurred, patiently waiting for my husband... This was not in our fate, though.*

Exhausted, they walk through the back alley that leads to the house, avoiding people, ready to sit down to rest and process what's happening. The group comes up to the back gate of their home; though not fancy, it is their one-level three-bedroom dwelling. The backyard is small but cute with a greenhouse in the corner and a detached garage that they enter from the alley. As they walk through the gate she hears Baby Girl barking to greet everyone and sees her jumping up and down, wagging her tail with a grin, looking at the group through the sliding glass door.

Casey hurries through the entryway and lets her pit out as she rushes in, hoping to see her husband.

Her heart drops, looking around and seeing an untouched house with no sign of Devon. She glances at the Christmas tree and all the decorations placed around the home. *It feels like a lifetime ago that I thought about Christmas; but, in reality, it was just earlier today. Will we even do it this year? My life is so uncertain. I just hope my husband can make it here.* Linc sits down on their brown love seat, his eyes heavy from the exhaustion. Walking over to him, she picks him up and takes him into his dinosaur-themed bedroom.

Laying Linc on his bed, she wraps him in his favorite blanket, pulling it up to his chin, and then kisses his forehead, watching her son's eyes slowly start to close. Slight smiles indicate he accepts the comfort of his room, and he quickly drifts off into a peaceful sleep.

"I love you, baby boy," his mother whispers into her sleepy son's ear and brushes her fingers down the side of his cheek.

Walking back into the dining room, she sees Jamie, who appears worn out. Casey tries to flip the light switch on but nothing happens, so she turns it back off. Seeing her friend without her carefree attitude worries Casey. Tall and thin with fair skin that shines in the sun, Jamie's crystal-blue eyes usually twinkle every time she smiles. She missed her call to be a model, living in this midwestern state, but right now her eyes do not twinkle, they just stare at the table as she is lost in her own thoughts. Casey walks to the cabinet in the kitchen and grabs water bottles for both of them, then sits down next to her, placing one of the waters in front of Jamie while watching both of the dogs settle down in the living room.

"Hey," she says slowly. "Are you OK?" Then she takes a sip of her water.

Jamie looks at Casey with such a troubled expression and then lowers her eyes again, her lips tight, too afraid to say what she is thinking. *Of course she's not OK. I'm not fine, but I did not know how to ask her what happened before she jumped into the dumpster.*

Looking down at the table for a few minutes, she finally lifts tear-filled eyes and says, "Today I met my parents to have a lunch date and shop. I had been so busy with work and finally made some time to see them at the little Italian restaurant on Main Street, when the lights went out. Sitting there for a while, thinking that the electricity would turn back on, I kept checking my phone, frustrated it was not working. Finally, we decided to leave and joined the people who were standing outside. Eventually, after talking with some of them on the street, we walked to the parking lot to see if we could get our car to turn over, when the vehicles came through. Once we heard the guy on the tank talk about the electricity being out everywhere my dad said we should stay together and go where it was warm. He thought that it was better to listen and get help, so we got in line to get onto a bus."

"While standing behind my parents, waiting to get on, the soldiers started shooting everybody! They hit both of my parents, and my father fell on top of me, forcing us to the pavement and knocking the wind out of me. That was when I felt his blood dripping all over! I do not know if he was trying to protect me or if he just fell; either way, he saved my life." She takes a deep breath and releases it, trying to control her trembling voice, and then continues: "I turned my head and saw my mom on the ground next to us with blood all around her. I watched her trying to breathe as she pulled her hand over to mine along the pavement and grabbed my fingers, lightly squeezing them. Seeing the tears stream down her eyes, I counted every breath she took until her last gasp for air… only nine times."

Gazing at the table, she struggles to continue. "After the soldiers passed by us, I let go of Mom's hand, shoved my father off, got up, and ran behind the buses for protection. Crossing over to the alley, I finally saw a dumpster where I could hide before they checked the area. I would have died too; they killed for no reason! Only explanation that I am alive is because my father took the bullet. I felt his chest rise up and down, and he whispered through painful breaths that he loved me; then he stopped!"

Watching the tears descending down her face, Casey thinks, *What a terrible thing to go through. How could she lay under her dad knowing that he was dying? This image must be haunting, repeating over and over in her mind: struggling to be quiet as her parents passed away and then having to leave them behind. I could never be that strong!*

Getting up, she goes to her room and finds clean clothes to replace Jamie's blood-covered apparel. It is the only thing she can do to help. Standing up, Jamie grabs her buddy, giving her a hug, breaking down in full-fledged tears, grieving all the pain and sorrow of the day. Casey struggles to keep her emotions together, knowing her friend needs someone strong right now. Finally Jamie lets go, trying to pull herself together, grabs the garments and bottle of water, then rushes to the bathroom to clean up.

Waiting for Jamie, Casey sits down and thinks, *Why are they messing with our town? Don't these soldiers have other cities to take over instead of meddling with this little nobody area? This is not some special realm with significant purpose that will help take over the country, not a big city like New York or LA. Maybe they are taking over those, too. I am sure now that I have to protect the little bit of family I have left. With so much to process, maybe if I had watched the news, we would know how in the course of one day our life went from being normal to being turned upside down! I went from happy housewife getting ready for Christmas to whatever this is. I mean, is this war?*

Looking at Jamie, who is now out of the bathroom and sitting at the table, Casey can see she has her tears under control and is in clean clothes. Watching her friend, she thinks, *Jamie is lost in her own horror story, as I'm trying to push the images out of mine. What about the poor man that was the first one to get shot? I swear he was looking right at me, with his mouth open, gasping in pain. He must have asked questions they did not like or did not want to go on the bus. Once he rejected the soldiers they got mad and started the attack.*

No, I can't think about that, her brain runs. *I must create a plan and think about my son. He is the only thing that keeps me thinking forward to the future and not what's happening in the present. What can I do to help my sweet, ex-*

hausted child who listened so well today? He was probably scared out of his mind. What else would silence a carefree spirit? Today would make any kid withdraw to some hidden place in their mind. Closing her eyes, she thinks, *1, 2, 3…*

"I have some items my husband packed in a couple of hiking bags. I think we need to get out of town. We have a cabin in the hills that my husband built, and it has an underground shelter on the land with a lot of supplies. If we can make it there, it would give us some time to think about what we need to do."

Am I really saying this to her? Can we make it? I mean, it's a very long walk for a child and two women. Will we die out in the cold winter? The underground shelter was something my husband insisted on making; plus, we bought supplies to stock it. How did he know we would need it? I need him so badly.

Jamie continues in silence, making Casey insecure about what she just said. Then, laughing quietly under her breath, Jamie says, "How would we get there? Walk? Even if we could make it to the hills, we must be able to survive the journey. We could starve. And what about your son and the weather? It is very cold out there." She tries to rationalize this idea presented to her.

Thinking about what Jamie said, Casey's mind runs: *This idea is not to be taken lightly. We have as much chance of dying out in the woods as we do hanging around here. If we stay, I have a bad feeling that the buses and tanks will come back to get us or worse. If we leave before they come, the group has a fighting chance to survive.* Casey looks down the hall to her son's room, where he is in a deep sleep. *Yes, this is what my husband would do. He would go into the woods. He taught me to shoot and hunt. This is for Linc, and waiting to die is not an option.*

Looking back at Jamie, she says, "I would rather die trying to survive than to be picked off like chickens in a henhouse. Linc, the dogs, and I are going in the woods. You can stay if you want, but this is what we have to do."

Jamie barely blinks as Casey stands. Making up her mind, she goes into their spare bedroom and brings out two large hiking bags. Both are filled with items, set up by Devon of what he thought was important for survival. Going back and forth between the rooms, she grabs a sleeping bag, a bow and arrows, and lastly the guns with bullets. Pulling out plastic bottles of water, cans of food, and fruit, she picks out what she thinks could last for a while and creates piles on the floor in front of the kitchen table. Jamie stares at Casey in awe. *She must be wondering why I had all this stuff ready to go.* Lastly, she goes into her bedroom and grabs two small awkward bags and one adult-size backpack.

Sitting on the floor, she shuffles through the food and items, rearranging both bags and filling them up, when Jamie finally asks, "Why so many bags?"

"The two smaller ones are designed to strap to the dogs, and the backpack Linc will carry. Everybody will have to contribute if we have any chance of making this work."

Continuing to work, she straps the bow and the sleeping bag to the back of one of the hiking packs and then puts lighter items into the backpack that is meant for Linc. Lastly, she disburses the guns and bullets evenly between each hiking bag while thinking, *This is going to be tough. There is so much weight for each person, but I know as we eat the food they will lighten up some; and I figure, if we have to, we will just throw out items that are not needed.* After packing everything up she glances at Jamie, who still looks like she is contemplating this situation.

"Do you want me to grab some extra snow clothes?" she asks, hoping this will confirm if her friend is going. *I really hope she does. It would make my life a lot easier if there is another person to help watch my child.*

After a few seconds Jamie says, "Yes, I will go with you."

Standing up, Casey goes into her room and grabs snow pants, coats, gloves, and masks for Jamie and herself and then goes into Linc's room quietly in order not to disturb him and grabs the same apparel. Lastly, she takes their boots, bags, and snow clothes and lays them next to the sliding glass door in the dining room. Everything has been packed to the best of her ability.

"Mommy," Linc calls, getting up from his nap.

Walking down the hall, Linc rubs his sleepy eyes and sits down on his mom's lap at the kitchen table.

"Mom, where is Daddy?" he asks, sweetly resting his head against his mother's chest.

"He is still at work." *Though I know by now he is not and don't know what to say to my son, still hoping that Devon will walk through the door.*

"Will he be home soon?"

"I do not know, son. We will just have to wait and see."

It has to be around six or seven o'clock. The sun has been down for a while now, and it's getting colder inside the house. Going outside, Casey finds their burn pit, drags it into the house, then takes one of her wooden chairs and slams it into the ground until it breaks to start a fire.

"Son, can you put on your snow clothes, please?" He obeys without arguing—he must be getting cold—and, to her surprise, Jamie follows Linc, putting on her heavy clothes, as well. Once the fire is burning Casey also puts on her snow clothes, opens the window to let the carbon monoxide out of the house, then finds a can of beans in the cupboard and puts them in a pot over the fire. Grabbing the cookware, Jamie takes over to give Casey a break while Linc sets his chair up by the fire.

After sitting in front of the flames for a few minutes Linc complains, "When can we get the TV back? I want to watch cartoons. Cartoons are good."

"I have cards in one of the bags if you would like to play a game," his mother suggests.

"No, that's no fun. I don't like that," he says, and continues to stare at the burning wood.

Getting up, Casey grabs some bowls and spoons from the kitchen so they can eat. Not having to worry about the dogs because they still have food and water, the group sits around the fire eating their beans, lost in their own thoughts, staring at the flames. Watching them dance back and forth, Casey can see the orange blend into red. The coals have a vibrant glow of orange that brightens up, then darkens, giving a rhythmic motion that is very calming.

Gazing at the glow of the fire, she sees her son on the other side of the burn pit and thinks, *What am I supposed to tell him? Sorry we lost your dad? No. He died? No, I cannot tell him that. I did not see that happen, and I am not ready to admit that I will never see Devon again. His dad is a survivor; he will make it back to us. He may come through the door any minute, run to us, and give us as hug. He will know what to do to fix our situation and not question himself the way I do. My husband is so confident and calm in a bad situation. I'm always the one who panics and freaks out.*

Circling her beans in the bowl with the spoon, she continues to think: *How we are going to make it through the woods in the cold? It's not a good idea to leave at night. We should wait and see if my husband shows up. Tomorrow will be better. We can leave when it's warmer. Staying in the house is safer than being out in the elements. Maybe we can stay here, the electricity will come back on, and everything will go back to normal. Now that thought feels like a better dream than going into the woods.*

"What are we going to do?" Jamie asks, as she is finishing her bowl.

Linc has already found his way to the floor to play with some of his toy cars, and Casey watches him for a second. *He is so innocent, pushing his cars back and forth, then crashing them together.* He screams in delight and crashes them again. *I wish that I could be happy so fast. At least he is starting to act like a normal kid again.*

"I think we should stay here as long as we can for shelter, but as soon as we feel our life is in danger, we'll run outside in the backyard to the ditch where the creek is and follow it right up into the mountains."

Jamie looks into the fire and nods her head. "What is happening to us?"

Casey stares at Linc for a minute and says, "We are being attacked. I finally realized it must have been started by an EMP before they came into town."

"But what does that have to do with the vehicles and cell phones?" Jamie asks, trying to understand.

"All computer systems or computer chips in this area must have been fried by the EMP. That's what shut down our vehicles, electricity, and telephones. I don't know who they are, but they are after us," she says, as she stands up and walks around the house grabbing blankets and pillows to set up a bed on the floor next to the fire. Deciding to help, Jamie spreads the blankets out, making a big bed. Finding a pen and paper, Casey writes, "*We were here and now we are there,*" hoping if they leave, her husband will see the note and know where they went. Checking the bags one last time, she wants to make sure they are ready to go before the group lies down for the night.

Looking out the sliding glass doors into the night, she sees that the moon is full and bright, casting enough light that she can see the alley without using a flashlight. *Though it is cold out, it is not snowing, and hopefully tomorrow will be warm enough so what's left will melt away. I assume we will head out on our journey early in the morning. What a horrible wife I am to be thinking about leaving without waiting to see if my husband makes it home.* And for the first time in a long time she drops to her knees, closes her eyes, and prays.

"Lord Jesus, please protect us on our journey to the cabin, keep us safe and warm, and don't let us starve. Also, Jesus, let us make good decisions for this trip. Lastly, keep my husband safe and let us see him again. In Jesus's name... Amen," she whispers.

Walking back, she checks the fire as Linc lies down while Jamie is on her knees adjusting the pillows, when suddenly they hear a loud noise outside. Casey slowly stands up from a bent-over position, filled with fear throughout her veins, and her hair stands up on her neck. Jamie turns her head to the window in the living room, and Casey runs to the glass that is covered by the curtains, pulling them back far enough to peer out, and sees military vehicles driving down the street with buses following behind them. Moving at the same time, Jamie gets up and pours her water bottle on the fire to put it out, then hurries over to Linc, scoops him up, and rushes over to the door to help put on his boots and coat.

"They are coming!" Casey yells and rushes to catch up to the two who are gearing up to leave.

"Mommy," her son calls out, frozen, eyes growing in fear.

Putting on Devon's boots, Jamie moves like lighting as Casey jumps into hers with no time to tie them, so she shoves the laces inside her winter shoes. Her friend does the same with her laces, puts on her coat, and throws a bag on her back. Right behind her, Casey zips up her own coat while her buddy grabs the two smaller bags in one hand and Linc's hand in her other; and as fast as they can, they run out the sliding glass door to the gate. Putting on the other hiking bag, Casey grabs her son's backpack, trying to catch up. The dogs follow Jamie and are in front of Linc's mom, sensing something is not right. Running across the back alley, they slide down into the ditch that has a very small creek. Casey stops in just enough time not to slam her friend into the water before they continue to race quietly west toward the mountains. Following the stream behind the houses, they try to put as much space between them and whatever is about to happen on their block. Hearing gunshots makes them stop behind a thick mess of bushes and branches of trees near the water, attempting to hide. They are a few blocks away from their house, and Casey cups her hand around Baby Girl's mouth to shut her up, afraid she will bark at the gunshots and give them away. Jamie holds Linc tightly to her chest to protect him, and his mother pulls out one of her guns that she stashed in her pocket earlier in the evening and cocks it. They sit quietly for a few minutes with both of the dogs ready to attack, on all four paws and hair standing on end. Komodo lies low to the ground, knowing not to give them away since they have already done this once earlier today. Their pit is ready to jump at anything that comes near them; she is a bullet restlessly waiting to be shot, growling under her breath, wanting to get out of her owner's grip. Holding her dog's mouth, Casey's knuckles turn white, while her other hand is holding the pistol, ready to shoot. *With just a few blocks to go and a sloping hill, we will be in the Black Hills Forest, where the cover will be thick.*

Hearing someone screaming and running out of the house just above the ditch line, they listen to the sound of gunshots. The next thing they see is a body fall into the ditch a few feet behind them. Closing her eyes,

Casey tries not to look at the lifeless body that just fell. Jamie pulls Linc's head to her body to hide him from the horror. They continue to hear multiple shots above them. Trying to stay still but not fully understanding, they now know they have nowhere to go but into the mountains. Something deep inside Casey says they will not lie down and surrender to this madness; she will do everything in her power to survive.

Hearing the gunshots move further to the east, she lowers her pistol and slowly lets go of her dog. Baby Girl has calmed down now that the noise is farther away. Quickly and quietly Casey ties her boots and takes the two small bags from Jamie, strapping them on the animals. She then attaches the leashes to each of the dogs and glances at the group, who looks exhausted, and she sighs, relieved that Linc had a nap today, knowing now that this is going to be a long night. Everybody looks at Casey to tell them the next move. She closes her eyes, takes a deep breath, *1, 2, 3...* then opens them and looks back at her entourage.

"OK, let's start walking." She grabs her son's hand, leading the way out of town.

Chapter 4

Walking in the ditch line, almost out of the neighborhood, the group follows the creek uphill heading into the Black Hills, trying to get away from the house and into the thickness of the forest. *Our cabin is very far from here,* Casey thinks. *Trying to make this journey in the dead of winter seems impossible. The only positive thought that comes to mind is that this has been a very mild winter so far. If we can just have a few weeks of no snow and wind, we may have a chance. Wishing we could have waited until tomorrow when the sun will be out, but the enemy had different plans, which make me glad I had all of the bags together before we tried to go to sleep.*

Looking down at her feet, she tries to concentrate on not tripping. *It seems like, whoever these military people are, they are doing a sweep through the whole town and either taking people or killing them. Why would they do this? This is the second time we had a close call with them and barely got away. How many chances are we going to get before they catch us? If we can only make it to the thick of the forest, we just have to survive the elements, stay hydrated, and avoid starvation. I hope this is a good idea.*

They continue following the creek line in silence. Casey keeps expecting her talkative son to start speaking, but he doesn't. He keeps his head down, watching his steps. Baby Girl is leading with Jamie holding her leash and Linc by her side, followed by Casey, who is holding

Komodo's leash. She figures once they are far enough away from town they can let the animals off their chains.

The moon is bright tonight, and the air is cold. They can see their breath making formations of clouds. Listening to the crunching sound of the snow underneath their feet, Casey looks up at the clear sky and sees the Little Dipper. Directing her eyes to the end of the handle, she stares at the bright Northern Star. *This is good for night traveling, to keep track of which direction we are going. Man, my bag is so heavy, and I wonder how long I can carry all this stuff.* Looking forward she sees Jamie, whose head is down, concentrating on where she is putting her feet. *I am sure her bag feels just as weighed down.*

We are one sorry-looking group; if they find us, we would be easy picking. Knowing Baby Girl would take a bullet for them makes her feel better. More aggressive than Komodo and constantly worrying about her people, she is teaching him to be that way as well. Casey puts a lot of trust in her to help when she needs it, though she knows that her dog is hot tempered and it is hard to control her barking. She continues to touch her pit's ears to see if her pet is getting too cold.

Steadily climbing for some time now, the hill gets steeper. Finally, they come across a small ridge they need to get over. Jamie helps the dogs get to the top, then takes her bag off and climbs up herself. Once she is there Casey hands her both bags. Grabbing Linc, she hands him to her friend and climbs up. Once on top she grabs her pack and looks around to see a small waterfall that is pooling up before falling over the ridge they just climbed. *We are definitely in the woods now. I can't see any more houses, and I wonder how far we have gone.*

Slowing down with heavy steps, Jamie turns around to look at Casey. "Do you think we should stop?"

Casey glances around to see what is nearby them and then steps away from the stream. "If we do, I do not want to be right next to the water. Do you think we are far enough away from town?"

The group follows her, and Jamie opens her mouth. "I don't know. Maybe if we are in the thick of the trees, we can get up early tomorrow and get out fast."

Pushing tree branches away from her face, Casey knows Linc is exhausted. Once they have walked far enough away from the creek, they search for a place to camp and come across a clump of bushes. *This spot is as good as any, in between these overgrown plants where we can put up our temporary home. I sure hope no animals come upon us.*

Setting her bag down, she digs into it and pulls out a small two-man tent, then grabs a collapsible shovel, puts it together, and starts to shovel the thin blanket of snow away to make a spot for their home. As she is doing this Jamie pulls the tent out of its case to have it ready to put in the spot that Casey is clearing.

"What are we doing here?" Lincoln asks after watching them work for a few minutes.

Casey stops her efforts while Jamie continues setting everything up. Sitting down on a rock, she pulls her son onto her lap. "We are all going to camp here tonight," she says, trying to sound excited about the situation.

Looking frustrated, he narrows his eyes at her. "How is Daddy going to find us way out here? He won't be able to."

Holding Linc tightly and giving him the best hug she can, Casey looks over his shoulder, watching Komodo walking over to them and sitting down in the snow at their feet. "I left Daddy a secret message at the house, so when he gets there he will know where we are and come to meet us."

Feeling a heavy weight in her chest, she closes her eyes. *I left my husband behind. Would he have left us? Probably not; he is the hero type. I just ran and now may never know if he is alive or dead.* A rush of sadness flows through her body. *I am a horrible person. Will he understand why we had to get out of town so fast? He would have done the same thing. I had no choice. I would have stayed and waited if they had not come and pushed us out.*

Pulling her head away, she looks at her son with tears filling her eyes. *My poor child... so confused and sad. Life is cheating us all, and now we are all stuck somewhere in the middle of the woods trying to make the best of this horrible situation. So many people died today, bringing us out here, and I am sure people are still being killed. Our only hope at this point is that the tanks are too busy in town to pay attention out of town.* The sadness washes over her again, making her body feel even heavier. *I'm no hero, just a survivor, not even good at that; more like a person who is squeaking by.*

Standing up, she grabs Linc's bag and looks through it to find his teddy bear. His eyes twinkle a little when he sees it, and she gives him a sad smile, knowing she found a way to make him somewhat comfortable for the night.

"Oh Mommy, he is my favorite bear. Oh, thanks!" He squeezes his bear close and rocks back and forth.

Getting up to help Jamie as she finishes the tent, Casey unstraps the sleeping bag, which is big and very bulky, adding a lot of extra weight to her pack, but she is glad they brought it. It is able to keep them warm in temperatures up to thirty degrees below zero. Casey shivers. Now that they have stopped walking she can really feel how cold it is. *It must be twenty or thirty degrees. I am sure happy we have snow clothes to deal with this. Plus, we all have an underlayer of clothing of long-sleeved shirts and long johns.* The adults roll out the sleeping bag in the tent as Linc sits outside on a rock with his dogs, patiently waiting and holding onto his bear. Once it's set up in the tent, Jamie takes off her boots and snow gear and then gets inside the bag to warm up.

"Lincoln, let's go to bed," Casey says and leads him into the tent.

After taking off his boots and snow outfit, he hops into the sleeping bag. Jamie scoops him in her arms and kisses him on his forehead. He grins, welcoming the comfort. Once all the hiking packs are put at the bottom near their feet, Casey lets the dogs in. She pulls out her husband's rifle and shotgun, then takes off her snow clothes, and gets in the sleeping bag. Sitting in it, she takes the packs off both dogs. Komodo lies down on the bags at their feet while their pit tries to curl up in Casey's arms under the sleeping bag. She does not zip up the bag and grabs her dog, wrapping an extra blanket around her to make sure she is fully covered.

Casey lays there for a few seconds, thinking, *The guns are in reach if I need them, the dogs are in front of the door, and Linc is between Jamie and me. I think this is as safe as I can make it for us tonight.* She whispers into the darkness, "I am glad you are here with us, Jamie. I don't know if I could have done this by myself."

"I am glad I ran into you in the dumpster, because I do not want to be alone. This is more of a plan than I ever would have thought of. I probably would have just given up and gone wherever they are taking everybody else," Jamie says.

Drifting off into sleep, Casey cannot take any more. Her eyes are heavy, though she tries to keep them open; and with her body tingling, she realizes how achy she is. *I'm not trained for this.* As striking pains attack her shoulders and with her legs feeling like jelly, she melts into the sleeping bag. *I hope my body will recover some overnight, because our journey has just begun and we have a long way to go.*

"Jesus, help us sleep well through the night and wake up in the morning. Please let us not starve, and keep my husband safe. Amen," she quietly mumbles to herself before falling asleep.

Chapter 5

The sun is bright in front of my eyelids, and I feel a warm liquid beside me that is very soothing. Opening my eyes, fluttering them into focus, I wake up and turn my head to see a body next to me. Sitting up and lifting my hand, I see blood dripping from my fingertips. At once I jump to my feet, trying to understand what is going on, and I see warm liquid pooling nearby and people all around me, shot and dead. Hearing groaning and moaning, I glance around to see their eyes are opening and they slowly sit up. They look at me and I see the anger in their faces, the tormented souls of the massacre. The girl in the alley with long, dark hair is staring at me, with blood running down her face and out of her coat, dripping from her hands. She yells at me, "Help, Help!"

Stepping back, I walk away from her. "Sorry, I can't, I can't!"

She yells for protection and reaches out for me, then narrows her eyes when I don't reach out to help her. Another person behind me grabs at my ankles and hollers for help. I pull my ankle away, but he does not let go. Kicking him, I hit him with the heel of my shoe right in his face, and his skull busts open and splatters blood all over me. But he did not let go of my leg. Struggling to pull away, I look around to see all the people are trying to reach for me, wanting me. They grab me, holding on so I cannot move, and it feels like they are trying to break my legs. The pain is horrible, shooting through my nerves. I look down to see blood is pouring from all the bodies surrounding me and *soaking into my shoes! The liquid is incredibly hot, like lava burning my feet, and my skin feels like it is on fire, peeling off.*

Then, looking up, I see my son screaming for me, crying in horror, standing about ten feet away in a group of bloody bodies, as the dead, gory people grab at him!

"Mommy, Mommy, help me!" he screams as loudly as he can, which cuts into my soul! The terrified screams of my child pierce my ears, trying to pop out each eardrum. The blood is surrounding him under his feet, and the dead are pulling his little body down, yanking at his legs! I must get to my son! I must save him, so I dive in his direction to help, but the dead people hold on to me.

"Lincoln!" I scream at him as loudly as I can, as I fall to my knees, trying to pull my legs up to get to him, but the dead are holding me down. I can see my son but cannot get to him. He is crying as he is being pulled down. His screams puncture my heart. I need to get to him! My hands are on the pavement, trying to fight being pulled to the ground. The blood is overflowing onto them, and the pain from the red liquid is all over, setting my nerves on fire. I'm dead and I cannot save my son. The people grab my shoulders now, making me submit to their misery. I can feel their fingers smearing the red liquid all over me as they get me closer to the ground. The blood is burning my skin off with searing pain, while I try hard to keep my eyes on my son, my precious child. Until finally I cannot see him anymore and I am completely engulfed by the bodies and the blood. The echo of my son's screams bounce in my eardrums, back and forth, as everything goes dark.

...

Suddenly Casey is awake, sitting straight up, looking for her child to make sure he is safe and by her side. Sweat is dripping down her face, and she is breathless. Linc is sleeping soundly. Realizing that it was just a dream, she tries to calm down and catch her breath. It was just a terrible nightmare with horrible images of dead bodies from the massacre. She thinks her dream was trying to punish her for leaving them behind, for surviving. Working hard to control her breathing, she lifts her shaking hand and lightly brushes her son's hair with her fingers to make sure he is OK.

The sun is burning brightly through the tent as she bends over and kisses her child on his forehead and sees his little chest go up and down, which makes her smile. *He is still alive. I wish I could have helped the other people, but I just am not strong enough. I am just barely holding it together as it is.* Watching her son and Jamie, who are still wrapped up together, lost in their own dreams, she thinks, *I sure hope they have better dreams than I just had!*

Both dogs open their eyes and watch what their owner is doing. She pats Komodo on his head, then Baby Girl's as well, so they know she is OK. Slipping out of the sleeping bag, she puts on her snow clothes and boots, then quietly steps out of the tent with the dogs following. The sun is bright and the warmth is inviting on her face. Looking around, she feels no present danger and is curious to see where they are and how far they walked last night.

The surroundings look a lot clearer in the day as opposed to last night. The tent is right in a mess of bushes and pine trees, and she sees they are not near any houses. The forest is thick with tall pine trees, and the smell of pine needles with morning frost engulfs her nose as she takes a deep breath. Casey closes her eyes and stretches while the dogs sniff around the ground and the plant life, getting to know the area.

Seeing that there is no present danger, she decides to let her group sleep for a while. Yesterday was so draining, and they need to build up as much energy as they can before starting today's journey.

Quietly she pulls one of the bags out from the tent and takes out a banana and water bottle, then sits down on a rock to eat. After finishing, she pulls out her map of the Black Hills and studies it. Finding the edge of town and the location of her house, she looks for routes that would lead them to her cabin located in the tiny town of Rochford in the heart of the hills. *The reality is that this is not going to be a walk in the park. It is probably going to take us a couple of weeks to get to the cabin, and we do not have enough food to last that long. Plus, we are not survival experts. What if we get lost?* She is glad to have a map, but she is still nervous about this journey. Her husband set them up with the tools they needed to survive, but she questions whether they will be able to use them properly to make it to their destination. *We will have to see. It is not like we can go back into town.*

Casey pulls out a banana and a water bottle each for Linc and Jamie and grabs some bread to give to the dogs. Tossing the food to the ground, the dogs scarf it down immediately. She readjusts her bag so it is ready to go and sets up each dog with their backpacks. Originally, they bought these bags for the dogs so they could carry their own water when the family went hiking. But now the bags hold a small amount of other items for the journey. Both have their own collapsible water bowl that flattens when it is not being used and some canned food. Komodo's bag also has a first aid kit just in case someone gets hurt so they can get to it right away. The thin layer of snow is starting to melt, and the wind is quieter, with just a slight breeze that she can barely feel. *Thank God*, she thinks.

Jamie finally comes out of the tent as quietly as she can so as not to wake up Linc, and looks around to assess where they are before she sits down next to her friend, who gives her a banana and water.

She peels her banana. "We didn't make it very far out of town, did we?" Then she takes the first bite of her food.

Still looking at the map, Casey finally looks up and says, "No, I guess just enough to not be shot. If I am looking at this right, by going a little east we should run into the main road that drives into the mountains. As long as we can stay hidden and follow that road we should get pretty far without getting lost."

"Do you think they will be driving on the road?"

"Maybe, but if we can at least see the road, I can tell exactly where we are on the map. I also have a four-wheeling map that shows the off-road trails. If we can see where we are, we can then head to the closest trail that follows it out to Rochford."

Jamie nods her head in agreement that they should at least check where they are on the map, and drinks some water. After a few seconds of eating and drinking she says, "Thank you for saving me yesterday."

Casey pulls her eyes away from the map and looks at her friend. "You saved yourself. I am glad we ran into each other, though. Now my son and I are not by ourselves. I really need somebody to help us get to the cabin, and I still do not even know if it was the right decision to escape through the woods. Jamie, I am sorry about your parents."

Jamie reaches over and hugs Casey tightly. "You are not alone. I know you were hoping that your husband would make it home, and I'm sorry he didn't. But again, you are not alone; we will figure this out together. We'll just have to stay strong for your son."

Tears well up in Casey's eyes as she tries to hold back her emotions. The first lesson in survival is being able to hold it together and not fall apart, which is very hard for her, but she pushes the sorrow down into her gut and smiles weakly at her friend. Just to know that she is not alone makes her feel a little better. *Maybe we can actually do this.*

Linc starts to moan in the tent, so she hurries in to grab him. Picking up her son, she hugs him tightly, letting him feel her strength and safety. She pulls him out of the sleeping bag to get his clothes on, and they come out of the tent. Then Jamie immediately goes to work rolling up the sleeping bags.

"What are we doing, Mom?" He rubs the sleep from his eyes.

"We are hiking today. This will be fun. It will be our own adventure with Jamie," she says to him in the happiest voice she can.

"I want to go home and see Daddy."

She hugs her son tightly again. "I want to see Dad too, but he is not at home and we are safer out here. We have to stay away from the bad guys."

He flashes frustrating eyes at her but decides not to argue. Linc pets Komodo, who is sitting near their feet, and takes a banana and water bottle from his mom without looking at her. Then she gets up to help Jamie disassemble and pack up the tent. Once done she straps it and the sleeping bag to her hiking pack and puts it on before helping Linc with his bag, and Jamie takes care of her own. Then they start walking toward the road.

After following a trail up a steeply sloping hill for what seems like a few miles, they finally make it to the top, where there are big granite boulders. Linc sits down on a rock, and his mother helps him open his water bottle. Then she pulls out the dogs' bowls and fills them with water. Jamie sets down her bag to join Linc while Casey looks for her binoculars. Since the group did not get far last night, she knows they are near the main road that leads out of town.

Stepping away from the group, she lies down on her belly between two big boulders and looks through the binoculars to see where they are. The bending road below confirms her fears. They did not make it far at all. The road is calm and quiet. She knows right where they are because she has driven this road so many times before, heading out to the lake. Putting down her binoculars, she feels her Pyrenees slowly nudging up next to her. He gets on his belly, and she turns to look at him, smiling as she pets him on the head. The small things in life make her feel a little better. The comfort from her dog is reassuring, even if it is only for a second. She leans her head into his fur, and Komodo licks her hair and neck. She giggles and then suddenly hears a noise from below. The sound immediately brings her back to the reality of the problems that they are facing. No more happy moment.

Quickly pulling her head back, she picks up the binoculars to look down at the road where she sees military vehicles heading into town. She counts eight vehicles and six buses. Many people are stuffed into the buses, looking overcrowded and miserable. She puts the binoculars down so they are hanging from her neck and creeps slowly on her belly back from the cliff, behind the boulder, to safety. Komodo follows by slithering in the same army-crawl style until he is behind the rocks with his owner. He sits up panting, and she hugs him around the neck. After a second or two they get up and head back down to the group, feeling very concerned. She can see that Jamie and Lincoln are sharing half of an apple.

"Well, what did you see?" Jamie asks, while she takes a bite and hands the apple to Linc.

"I saw the main road, and we are very close to town. I also saw military cars and buses carrying people out of the mountains."

"I wonder where they are taking all the people."

"I don't know, but I do not think this is good at all. They are forcing people to go with them. That is why they were shooting yesterday. I saw a man run away from the buses, and he was the first person to be shot. It seems like they are making some kind of camp somewhere."

Now that she sees exactly where they are, Casey is no longer sure about following along the road, so she pulls out the map again. *If the military is going into the hills and pulling people out, we will be sure to run into them again. I wonder if there are some creeks we can follow?* She stares at the map, placing her fingers on the different streams to see how far away they are and whether any of them comes close to their destination. She finds one they can follow southwest, further away from civilization, which is deeper into the hills and not near any main roads, but they will have to follow the compass to get there.

"What do you think we should do? We can either follow the road or we could go southwest toward this creek." She points to the map where the stream is so Jamie can see it. "It is not a straight shot to Rochford, but we will be well hidden and have access to water. The journey will take many more days, but I think it will be safer than the main road."

She watches her friend decide on these options she presented. After a few minutes Jamie looks up at the sky and then closes her eyes, absorbing the sun. She opens them and looks at Casey. "I think we should head toward the creek. As you told us, we will be away from people and close to water. That's the best idea."

Casey nods her head and looks at the map again to make sure her bearings are straight. Looking at the compass, she says, "Then we need to go that direction, southwest." She points her finger in the direction they need to go.

Jamie nods her head and stands up to put on her bag. Linc has finished his food and is sitting in the snow, petting Baby Girl, who looks up alertly as the girls get up. Still holding his empty water bottle, Linc looks at it and throws it on the ground. Casey watches her son, and he glances at his mother while she picks up the bottle.

"Son, you need to remember that people will last only three minutes without oxygen, three hours in harsh elements, three weeks with no food, and only three days without water." She gives the bottle to him. "Keep it so when we are at the creek we can refill them all. Do you understand?"

His eyes wide open, Lincoln looks at his mom, amazed, trying to understand what she said; as does Jamie, who just stares with her eyebrows raised high. And thinking about it, Casey wonders the same thing. This information must have come out of some filing cabinet packed way in the back of her brain that has never been opened. *I must have seen this information on TV, or maybe I read it in my survival book. I read a couple of chapters but did not get very far before I lost interest. Sure wish I gave it more time now. But I did bring the book, so I will be able to read it when I find some time.*

Lincoln puts the empty bottle back in his backpack, and his mother helps him put his bag on. She also repacks the dogs' bags as they get ready to head out, hoping they can reach their first destination in one day.

"Look, Casey, look!" Jamie exclaims and points to the sky, toward the southeast.

Looking over her shoulder, she sees big clouds of smoke rising high into the sky. She ventures closer to the big boulders to get a better look and sees burning houses in parts of the west side of town near her neighborhood. *They are burning people out!* Linc steps up next to his mother and she pulls him closer.

"Are they burning our home?" he asks.

"Maybe. I can't tell." *The more I learn about these evil people, the angrier I get. This fight has just begun. They may just have burnt down my life and caught us off guard, but we will recoup, we will get stronger. I vow to myself we will fight back once we are ready.*

She mutters under her breath, "May Jesus bless you, Devon. Please stay safe, stay alive. In Jesus's name…"

Turning back to Jamie, she says, "Let's get going. We have a long way to walk, and we need to get as far away from town as we can." After a quick look at the compass again to make sure they are going southwest, they start walking toward the creek.

Chapter 6

Jamie leads the way down the hill toward the creek; Linc and Komodo are right behind her. Keeping an eye on her son, Casey watches his every step down the steep hill, with Baby Girl following at the end of the line.

About two miles into the hike, Linc says, "I'm tired, Mom. I want to rest and take a drink."

There are some good-sized rocks just ahead, and Casey points at them for her son to sit down. Digging in her bag, she finds a new water bottle for him and water for the dogs. As they rest for a few minutes she realizes this is going to be a long day if they stop every couple of miles.

"Son, are you ready, buddy?" Casey asks, while she puts the dogs' water bowls away.

"No, Mommy, I want to go home."

"We are not going home. We are going to our new home. Remember the cabin?"

"Oh, the cabin is our new home? What about my toys we left them behind? Do you think they burned?"

"Remember, you have toys at the cabin."

"Whatever! I want Dad!"

"I know. We will see him soon. I love you, and you just need to have some faith. We will see Daddy again."

"Ok, Momma, I will get some faith."

"Then we should get going," she says with a gentle smile.

Jamie keeps her head down, staring at the wet dirt from the melting snow, lost in her own thoughts, while Casey tries to get Linc going. *My strong-willed child is trying so hard to be brave. His belief of finding his father keeps him going. One day I will have to explain to him why I let him think this way. But as for now it works to get him up and walking.* She gets up, and Jamie follows suit but stays silent. It seems like every few miles they have to stop and Casey has to continually find ways to push her son. She really would like to make it to the creek and set up camp before night comes. It would be easier to set up the tent in daylight, as they are trying to avoid making fires that would let people know where they are.

For most of the day the group keeps walking, and Casey can see the sun starting to go down. The air is getting cooler; her breath is making clouds again. Night is getting ready to settle in; she wonders how much longer they have before it is completely dark. She checks her compass to make sure they are still going in the right direction, as it seems like they should have already made it to the creek.

"Maybe we should stop for the night and set up camp," Casey suggests.

"We might have another hour before the sun is completely down." Jamie looks through the trees into the sky. "I want to make it to the creek as much as you do."

She nods and keeps walking forward. Feeling tired from moving all day, their backs achy from the weight of the bags, the group keeps pressing on, believing that the creek cannot be that far away. *Nothing exciting happened today, which is a nice change from yesterday. If we can find some meat, then we have a good chance of making it to the cabin and can start over, hiding underground.*

As they work their way down a sloping hill they finally hear the trickling of the creek. The fresh smell of the water fills Casey's nose as she takes a deep breath and smiles in relief. Jamie can see the small stream through the trees, and she stops and turns back to look at her friend with a big grin on her face. *Destination one is complete*, Casey thinks. *We did it, we did not get lost, and I can checkmark this portion off the map.*

"Hey guys, this is a flat spot here on this hill. Let's make camp so we are not too close to the creek," she says happily.

Jamie nods her head with her eyes twinkling. This is the first time since they met in the dumpster that she has actually seen a smile on her friend's face, with eyes so bright she could melt any man's heart. There is still some sunlight left in the day, and it feels good to have some success after such stressful events took over their lives.

They work hard to get camp set up before nightfall. Casey pulls out some cans of fruit with almonds to eat for dinner and opens one can of beans for the dogs. It is not much food for everybody after a long day of walking, but she wants to ration it to make it last as long as they can.

"This food is no good, Momma. I want pizza," Lincoln says sadly, looking at the can in disgust.

"I know, buddy, but this is what we have."

He finally starts to eat, slowly accepting the truth that they are not at home anymore. All of them have to be satisfied to eat what they have because there are no grocery stores around here. Once he finishes eating Linc pulls his teddy bear out of his bag and goes into the tent. Casey pulls out the map to find their next destination. It shows the creek leads up to Sheridan Lake where they need to go next. Once they go around the lake they can follow the road behind it that will lead them to the back trail that goes to Rochford. She assumes it will take many days to get to the lake. But she is only guessing at this point. The weather and her son will determine how fast they can move. Since they are following the creek, there will be plenty of water to drink. Hopefully she can find them some food. Even with rationing, the little food that is left will not last the whole trip.

Jamie is drawing in the mud with her foot, enjoying the rest after a long day of walking. Both of the dogs are lying down, watching over them, and the sun is almost all the way down, ready for the night.

"Tomorrow morning, I am going to get up early and try to hunt. Could you watch Linc and Baby Girl?" she asks.

"Yeah, that's fine. Is Komodo going with you?"

"Yes, I want him with me because he is more patient than my pit. Do you still have the gun I gave you?"

"Yes, I hope that you get something to eat because we do not have enough food to make it," Jamie comments, while still creating her mud art, not looking at her friend.

Then Casey digs in her bag and pulls out a book, piquing Jamie's interest. "Do you want me to read a bedtime story?"

Jamie laughs and says, "Let's do it."

Casey heads into the small tent and lies down next to her child, who is looking at his teddy bear. Jamie and the dogs follow her into the tent and lie down on the other side of her son. Casey zips up the flap and opens the book to start reading. A picture of her family falls out when she opens it; it's one of her favorites. Right away she sees Devon's face. His dark eyes almost look black in the picture, and his black hair and neatly trimmed goatee match the intensity. He is so masculine, with wide shoulders and muscular biceps that stand out in the tight shirt he is wearing. A slight smile shows he complied with this picture. Her child is as happy as can be, standing in front of his dad, whose strong hands are on his son's shoulders, trying to keep him still. Casey is standing next to her husband, with her brown hair and highlights with bangs that sweep to the side while naturally spiral-wavy hair hangs freely in front. She momentarily feels the moment when the photo was taken as she smiles at the picture with her brown doe eyes. She remembers trying to hide her big front teeth as she smiled. *What a great picture of my family*, she thinks. They had decided to take this family photo last summer to update their image of Linc, who was growing so fast. She had forgotten she must have put this extra copy in the book. As quickly as the warm memories appear, they leave. She stuffs the picture back in the book so her son doesn't see it and get upset about his dad.

"Matthew 1:1," she reads out loud from her Bible that she packed when her husband asked if there was one special item that she wanted to take if needed. She keeps reading until Linc is asleep and Jamie's eyes are closed. Before her eyes tire out she pulls the picture back out and stares at it for a while to bring back those memories.

. . .

I am running through the forest as fast as I can, hearing people coming from behind, trying to close in on me. They are going to catch me, I just know it. Looking toward a clearing in the thick of the trees, I stop right in my place. Am I seeing correctly? In the tall grass with wild flowers sprinkled throughout the small clearing is somebody I know, somebody I have not seen in a really long time. It is my Prince Charming, my tall, handsome husband, who is staring at me with his Indian black eyes! He is here to save me, to rescue me from the problems that are closing in. Running to him as fast as I can, I'm ready to jump into his arms. We collide and I fall into his embrace. Emotions sweep over me, and I begin to cry. He hugs me so tightly as I close my eyes. When I finally look up at his face I push back hard. Fear engulfs me as I see him decaying right before my eyes! His skin is turning colors of gray and brown to black in a rapid pace, and blood starts to stream down his face from his hair line and dripping out of his eyes like tears. He never stops staring at me! Stumbling, I try to walk backward after seeing my husband half dead and half monster! I cry out in pain from the torment of my life. "No, not my Devon!"

He looks at me with sad, dead eyes that are now narrowing as he says to me, "You left me behind. You did this! It is your fault!" He picks up his hand and points his finger at me with skin that is melting away, starting to show the bone of the tip of his finger. Then he raises all his fingers and tries to reach out for me.

"You can't run forever! They will find you; they will catch you!" He smirks and starts to laugh. Jumping back, I turn to run back for the woods. He jumps after me and lands on top of my body. He is so strong! I cannot get away. He turns me around where all I can see is his bloody skull with skin and red liquid dripping on my face. I close my eyes for protection. His whole body is turning into

nothing but bones and blood. He wraps his skeleton hands around my throat and starts to choke me....

...

Casey wakes rapidly, coughing and gasping to get air back into her lungs. It was a dream, only a dream, she tells herself. Beads of sweat drip down from her forehead from this terrifying nightmare. She looks over at her son and Jamie, still trying to control her breathing. Both of them are in a deep sleep. She hopes their minds are not haunting them the same way. She opens the tent flap to look outside.

The sun is peeking over the horizon. The ground has frost on it, but the snow is beginning to melt. Thank God, it has been a mild winter so far. They just might make it if the weather stays like this. She gets dressed in snow clothes and grabs the backpack that Linc normally carries. After emptying the items he had in it last night, she repacks it with supplies needed for hunting. Then grabbing her bow and arrows, she calls Komodo, ready to see what they can find for food.

Baby Girl tries to follow, but Casey pushes her back in the tent. Her pit looks at her sadly and starts to whine. "No, Girl, you cannot come. Love you," she says and zips up the tent door.

As they walk away from camp and into the woods, she tries to remember what Devon taught her about hunting. She needs to find a path that shows where the deer have been. After a few miles of walking, Casey thinks she has found a trail and looks around for a tree to climb into. A few feet away there is a big pine tree that has some branches low to the ground, one that she can climb and hide in. She ties a rope around the tree and her waist to keep her from falling, just in case. She readies the bow with an arrow that she chose to use so she can save their bullets. An arrow can be reused as long as she doesn't lose it, but once a bullet is shot it is gone forever. Komodo circles around the bottom of the tree until he finds just the right place to lie down.

The air is fresh and cool this morning, and Casey can see her breath creating clouds as she exhales. The birds are chirping, making it peaceful in the forest. This is far better than being in town with all the chaos. Since they started this journey it has been vital for her to succeed. Her son's life depends on it. With so much pressure on her to make the right decisions, she worries that if she makes the wrong choice, they could die, just as they probably would have if they had gone on the bus or stayed at the house. So far, they slid by under the radar to get here. She sure hopes they can keep getting by, and right now they need some meat. She is glad they made it out of town, but there is still so much danger around them. An animal could come upon them unexpectedly. Other desperate people could find and attack them. Or even worse, the military guys could be out here searching for people who have run away. To think they are the only ones in the woods would be naive. She is sure a lot of people ran for the hills. Two women and a child on their own are in a vulnerable situation.

After a few hours Casey starts thinking about her nightmare. It was a horrible vision of her husband's death. Deep down, she feels really guilty about leaving without knowing if he is OK. Somewhere in her mind she thinks if Devon is dead, it is her fault. And with this thought, reality settles in that there is a possibility she will never see her husband alive again. Tears roll down her face as she realizes the tragedy of what they are going through. The series of events that led them to be out here in the middle of the woods in the dead of winter keeps running through her head. If she only knew if he is alive, and if so, where, she thinks they could save him. Her mind is torn with conflict. How can she save Devon when she is barely able to help herself and her son?

She sits in the tree for what seems like forever, but nothing comes by. Komodo never leaves his spot in the dirt below. He is as quiet as can be, scanning the woods on high alert, making sure they are safe. After a while she decides they will have to try again tomorrow and climbs down. The dog gets up and stretches his legs out. Once she steps on the ground he nudges her hand with his nose to get attention. He sniffs her leg to make sure everything is OK, and Casey rubs the top of his head as he closes his eyes, enjoying the comfort. They walk over to where she set a couple of rodent traps last night to see if they caught anything. There is nothing, so she picks them up, puts them in her bag, and they head back to camp with nothing to show for the morning out, but she remains optimistic. They still have canned food, and this is the very first time she tried to hunt and trap. She is confident their time will come to get some meat and is hopeful that it will be before they run out of food.

By the time they make it back to camp, Jamie is packing everything up. She looks up, hoping for good news. Casey shakes her head no, and Jamie resumes her task. Once Linc sees his mother, he runs up to her with excitement, refreshed from sleeping.

"Mommy, Mommy, I thought you were gone forever like Dad!"

She shudders at his words of his father, but she can say nothing to make him feel better.

"Son, I am here, buddy. Mom will not leave you forever. I just went hunting. I will try to hunt every morning, and you will help Jamie pack up camp. OK?"

"Did you get anything?" he asks.

"Not this time, but maybe tomorrow."

Their new schedule begins, with Casey waking up before dawn trying to hunt and trap, which up 'til now has been unsuccessful. Then they walk as far as they are able every day, continuing to follow the winding creek up the hills to the west, trying to reach Sheridan Lake. As the days go by they seem to move slower. With very little food to eat, their bodies do not want to do so much work. Casey eats only once a day just so Linc can have a little more. In their old life, she would have jumped at the chance to go out hiking and camping. Now she is worn out and feels like a failure. It would be wonderful to sit in a warm tub of water and clean off. Feeling cold all the time, the chill has settled in her bones and has become her new normal. Casey thinks she should have listened more to Devon about hunting and surviving and should have pushed more to practice on her own so she could be more confident. Now she feels like they are completely at the mercy of God's grace to keep them fed. This is how cavemen must have felt: cold, tired, and dirty. If Jamie and Linc starve, it will be entirely her fault for dragging them out here, and her remorse will be unthinkable.

Lincoln does not say much anymore; he is turning inward with his thoughts. He fights every day to keep at the adults' pace, believing that Mom knows what she is doing. His childlike attitude is changing right before her eyes. There are fewer smiles, and he is much more serious due to the pain he has endured. The light in his face is dying down. Komodo can get a weak smile out of him, and sometimes Jamie can get him to laugh. But the young, vibrant six-year-old child is not here anymore.

They set up camp every night, and Casey checks the map and tries to find the best spot to set up the two small traps. She prays every time that they will get something, anything, to eat. After that they all sit down and feed on a very small amount of food—only one can for all three of them plus the two dogs. Finally, after their miserable meal, they go in the tent and read the Bible, trying to forget their hunger pains and fall asleep. Casey's stomach growls so loudly every night she can feel the echoes of vibration in her intestines. She thinks her stomach may just start eating itself if they do not find some food soon.

Chapter 7

By the seventh day of walking beside the creek, they're feeling really bad. Like turtles slowly pacing up the hill, every step takes all of Casey's energy to keep pushing forward. The hike feels like it continues forever. The weather has been the same for the last few days: cold but no snow or windy conditions.

On the hill they are walking up, the group comes across some big boulders blocking them. At the bottom of the boulders is a pool of water that has built up from spilling over the rocks. They can hear the rushing sound of the cascading water hitting the bottom of the pool. It must have just melted, because there is still ice built up around the sides. The smell of fresh water is overpowering as they look at the granite wall in front of them. Unfortunately, all this means is that they have to climb up the steep rocks somehow. Today Casey is leading the group, with the dogs following behind her. Linc and Jamie are lined up behind the animals, and everybody waits for Casey to decide the best way to get on top of the cliff. She stops to take a drink of water as she thinks.

"What do you want to do?" Jamie asks, while she is searching in her bag for a bottle of water.

Linc settles down on the ground while Komodo nudges him for attention. Baby Girl huffs and puffs as she sits to rest at her owner's feet, who scratches her ears for a few seconds while she scans the area. Finally, she spots a small cliff a little way from the water that looks like it almost has steps along the wall of the rocks that they may be able to climb up.

"Over there looks like the best way up." She points her finger at the ascending platforms.

"Alright, we can do this," Jamie replies and gets her bag back on.

Getting up, the group follows Casey over to the ledge of rock. She steps up onto the first platform, and the dogs join her. Jamie picks up Linc, and his mom reaches for him to bring him up also. Working their way up the rocks in this fashion, the dogs try to race their owner while she continues to make sure her son doesn't get hurt. On the last ledge she uses her upper body strength to pull herself up and over. Once on top she straightens herself up and turns her head to look around.

About ten feet in front of her is a big brown mountain lion staring her down! He is on the ledge of another boulder, looking very powerful and majestic. Suddenly he jumps off the rock right in front of her and starts to hiss. Casey sees him sizing her up, and she stumbles backward, startled, and falls on her back! She tries to hold her balance as she almost falls off the edge of the granite. Her head is hanging over the cliff. Using all the muscles in her neck to keep her head high, she takes her eyes off the mountain lion for just a second and looks over the edge she almost fell off; then she looks back. He is ready to attack her, bending his knees and digging his paws into the dirt, bracing the ground to use full force to jump on her. Right as he bends his knees a little deeper and licks his lips with a slight smile, Komodo jumps in front of his owner and starts to bark at the cat. Baby Girl is the next one to get up on the plateau of the cliff and positions herself to the left side of this ferocious animal. She starts to bark at the mountain lion to get its attention off her owner and onto her. The cat hesitates for a second, looking at both of Casey's dogs, trying to keep its eyes on all three of them. Pulling herself together, she sits up, regaining her composure, and grabs her gun, then cocks it. Pointing it right at the cat, she tries to get good aim, but the mountain lion is not ready to give in to its prey and hisses at her again, looking past the dogs. He shows no sign of fear and puffs his chest out, then digs into the dirt and looks at Komodo, ready to take him down in order to get to Casey. Her Pyrenees is ready and not willing to back down either. His knees bend and lock into position while he growls low and mean at this fearless animal. At that instant the cat jumps with all of its strength, paws stretched out, pointing his claws in front of him, ready to dig into her dog. Komodo jumps at the same time, ready to give the lion all that he has. Casey's gun is pointing right at the cat's head, and she squeezes the trigger. With a blast that yanks her hands back, the bullet jumps forward with mighty force. It shoots pass the dog, missing him by inches, and hits the cat right in its forehead. The clean shot stops the lion right in the air, and it falls to the ground. Her dog, still in mid-air, follows right behind the bullet and goes right for the throat of the cat. He lands on the animal and digs his teeth into him. The cat barely struggles to fight off Casey's dog. His paws go in the air, feebly attempting to push Komodo off, without success. By this time Baby Girl joins in and grabs the cat at the back of its neck, making sure it is dead.

Casey tries to catch her breath from her adrenaline rush. *I could have died! He may have been stalking us for a while, waiting for his chance to get us.* Sitting on the ground, she watches her dogs in such a vicious state. *Never have I seen this side of either of them. They were able to resort to their primitive instincts in order to save their owner.* That they could get this way scares her, but she is relieved that they were here and ready to die to protect her. *What love and loyalty these animals have for me, for us.*

"Hey! Are you OK?" Jamie yells as she gets on top of the rock.

She grabs Casey's shoulders from behind and watches the dogs' viciously attacking the mountain lion. Turning around, Linc's mom watches as Jamie pulls her son up on the rock. She sees his face as he stares at both dogs with his mouth open and fear in his eyes while trying to steady himself on the plateau. This causes her to get her breath under control and regain her composure for the sake of her child.

"Komodo, Baby Girl, come here now!" She tries to sound demanding, but her voice comes out shaky.

Both dogs hear their owner's command and come running to her side, and they sniff her to make sure she's OK. Then they go to Linc and Jamie to make sure they are fine, as well. Both animals wag their tails and prance around to show how strong they are. Casey sees the blood all over their mouths, and she has to turn away to pull herself together.

"Well, we have meat," she struggles to say and tries to smile at her group to make light of this situation.

Komodo comes over again and lies down on the ground by her feet, staring at the cat, while her pit circles around the dead animal, checking their surrounding area to make sure they're safe. Linc steps over to his mom and sits down on her lap. Jamie steps in front of her friend and bends down, balancing her weight on her knees, and makes eye contact.

"Are you OK?"

Casey takes a deep breath and hugs her son. "Yeah, the dogs saved me. I just barely got a shot off after they distracted the cat."

"What do we do now?"

"I want to field dress it and cook it so we can eat well tonight." She kisses Linc's hair with a slight grin on her face.

Jamie smiles back and laughs, shaking her head. *What a blessing from God to send a mountain lion our way. He literally put meat in front of my face, which we need since we only have a few cans of food left.*

"When I cook the meat I do not want the fire near our camp because the smoke trail will lead to where we are sleeping. Can you take Linc and Baby Girl with you to set up the tent a few miles in that direction?" She points into the trees to the north. "This way, I can take care of the meat, and I will haul it back to you guys."

Jamie smiles at her friend and nods her head. Then she jumps up, ready to contribute to the task at hand. *She has been such a big help, coming with us. I appreciate her willingness to watch Linc and help the group.*

"Are you sure you will be fine by yourself?" she asks one last time.

"Yes. Lincoln, Mommy is going to take care of this animal. I want you to go with Jamie and help her set up the tent. I will be there in a few hours. OK, honey?" Then she hugs her son.

"I will help her. She is my friend." He stands up and grabs Jamie's hand with admiring eyes.

They walk to the north, and Linc looks back at his mom, waving his hand with a slight grin on his face; she smiles and waves back. Baby Girl is trailing behind the group, understanding now that it is her job to stay with them. Casey watches all three walk away until she cannot see them anymore, glad to see her son and friend have become so close. Then she turns and looks at the mountain lion in front of her and sees Komodo still lying in the dirt right near it.

The cat has light-brown fur with a white face and gray highlights around the mouth and ears. His eyes are surrounded by black hair, like someone painted eyeliner on him. His dark-blue marble eyes stare at Casey, and she cannot help but stare back; his face is so commanding. She can't believe her dogs were brave enough to stand up to this amazingly beautiful creature.

Taking a deep breath she thinks, *1, 2, 3...* and opens her bag to find the hunting knife kit. She also pulls out her parachute rope and a few more items, setting them down on the dirt next to the lion. Getting on her knees, she looks over at her dog, who moves around to find another spot to settle down in the grass a few feet away. Casey has field dressed a deer before, but this is the first time she will cut into a mountain lion.

She puts her hand under the belly of the lion and pushes him over on his side, feeling his fur and thinking it is soft like a fleece blanket. Once she gets him in a good position to cut into his belly, she takes her knife and pierces the skin. The blood starts to drain out of his stomach and drips down his side, pooling onto the ground right underneath his body. Positioning herself so the blood does not flow toward her, she starts slicing through the skin down his belly to open up the cavity and closes her eyes when she puts her hand inside to pull the organs out. Once everything has been removed she gets up and walks over to the creek to wash off. Next she throws the rope over a tree branch right above her. After tying one end around the lion's body under the front legs, she grabs the other end and pulls the carcass up into the air until it is hanging at a good height to cut the meat.

Before Casey begins, she sits down to rest and stares at him hanging in the air. *Should I keep the fur?* she wonders. *If I remember right, I need to stretch it and dry it out. We have clothes and we need the meat, so I guess I don't think the fur is important at this moment.*

She looks around for some rocks to make a burn area, while some of the blood drains out of the lion. Stacking them up in a circle to create a contained area for the fire, she builds the walls up on both sides and places a long slate rock across the top of the pit where she can place the meat to cook. Then she stacks tree branches and pine needles in the pit, thinking they will catch fire easily. Pulling out some grocery bags, Casey places them neatly near the fire for the meat once it is cooked. Lastly, she grabs her magnesium fire starter. Deciding she has everything ready, she goes back to the mountain lion and starts to cut off its fur.

Once the fur is gone Casey washes her hands and grabs her knife to scratch the magnesium until she has the silver flakes on top of her tinder. Taking her knife, she scrapes the flint, which makes sparks, and after several minutes she finally creates a small flame. Smiling to herself, she thinks, *Good job, Casey,* feeling good she remembered something her husband taught her. *He would be so proud of everything I have accomplished. I killed the mountain lion with the help of my dogs, then field dressed it, dealing with the blood and organs, and now I've started my own fire.* She bends over to the small flame and lightly blows on it to give it more oxygen. The flames catch and climb up the tinder to the branches.

Standing up, she starts cutting off the first backstrap while the fire is warming up. Slicing into the meat, she curves the knife down along the spine of the mountain lion. Concentrating on cutting, her arms shake as she saws at it, trying to ignore the sharp pains in her shoulder blades. Tired from all the work that she done, she keeps telling herself that Linc needs this meat and he needs her. Finally, she gets the first piece cut and lays it on top of the slate before continuing to cut more.

Smoke from the fire soars high in the sky. All Casey can think is that it is a perfect gray, black puffy trail that leads right to her. She is sure that the enemy can see it and is concerned they will come this way to see what is burning in the hills. *I am glad I told Jamie to set up camp away from here and hope that it is far enough that they will not be found. Plus, I showed her how to use a gun, so they do have some protection, and they have Baby Girl, too. She will attack anything that is not supposed to be near them.*

Casey turns the meat and looks down at Komodo, who has been following her every move. He knows he is on guard duty right now and is not ready to rest. Watching him peer into the woods, checking in all directions, she pets his soft, fluffy, thick fur. He welcomes the comfort and points his nose to the air while closing his eyes for a second.

Once the last piece of meat is cooked she wraps it in the grocery bag and puts it in the backpack. She dumps the rest of her water on the fire to put it out, wanting to get out of here as fast as she can, afraid the enemy is on their way. The air is colder now, and Casey can see that the sun is going down. Walking in the direction that Jamie went earlier, she tries to move fast but is tired from all the day's work. As the darkness settles, she feels more nervous about just the two of them walking through the woods. She prefers more people in a group so she is not such an easy target. Komodo is on high alert, with his ears pointing straight up and stretching out to pick up every sound wave that comes by. He does not want to miss anything. She listens intently too, and thinks, *I swear I can hear so much more out here on my own. Every twig we are stepping on cracks.* Tiptoeing through the woods, she can feel her calves burning from holding all her weight in this position.

After a few miles of walking, the sun has gone down. It is now completely dark, and she feels the bitter cold settling in for the night. Uncertain how far away camp is, Casey starts to focus on her breath. Seeing the puffy white clouds coming out of her mouth makes her think, *I must make it back to my son*, which keeps repeating in her head. She is sure both Jamie and Linc are worrying about her, and she hopes to find the tent soon but realizes that her friend took her words to heart and walked quite a while before they stopped to set up camp. Her mind races: *Linc has lost one parent already; he cannot lose me too!*

Casey's stomach is growling, and she can feel the vibration of the wall of her belly crawling, begging for the food it knows she has. Not wanting to eat any meat until she can be with her group and celebrate their victory together, she tries to ignore her tummy. Even though the mountain lion fell in her lap, Casey is proud that she was able to kill, clean, and cook it. Now they can last a few more days, maybe even a whole week, just on the meat and not have to eat any of the canned food that they have left. Since they do not eat as much food, it should last longer. *If we can get a few more animals and stay hidden, we may just make it*, she thinks. This mountain lion has just raised her morale, if she can only make it back to camp with the others. They should have a great day tomorrow.

Feeling like it has been forever tiptoeing through the trees, she can barely see ahead of herself in the darkness. The moon fades in and out behind the clouds, but at least the wind is calm tonight, and she welcomes the stillness. Casey keeps her head down most of the time to watch where she's putting her feet; and being that it is night, she is more cautious, not wanting to trip and get hurt. She would be in a lot of trouble if that happened, and feels like one wrong move could kill Linc, Jamie, or even herself. These pressures cause her to slow down and really think about every decision she makes, as each one could determine if they live or die.

Through the clearing of trees, the moonlight shines between two clouds, and she finally sees the white and black spots of her pit lying in the dirt in front of some bushes. It is like God just shined his flashlight down to direct Casey to her camp. Baby Girl perks up her ears, hearing them walk through the trees. Their footsteps broke the silence of the night and put her on guard. Komodo obediently follows behind his owner, but when he sees his friend he sprints ahead to meet up with her. Her pit barks and charges at them. She is ready to attack until she realizes that it is her family, and meets her buddy halfway between Casey and the tent. Both dogs are happy to see each other, licking and sniffing each other with their tails wagging. Once she is done checking on Komodo, Baby Girl runs to her owner, happy to see her also. Bending over, she pets her dog to let her know she is fine. Her pit gives her owner the biggest smile across her face, she is so glad to see them.

The noise disturbs Jamie and the quiet of the woods. Casey stands up and approaches the tent as it is unzipped. Jamie points the shotgun out of the door flap first, and then she pokes her head out to see who it is.

"Casey, is that you?" she asks nervously.

She turns her head in Casey's direction and smiles in relief. Lowering her gun, she steps out of the tent to greet them and hugs Casey tightly. Glad to be back with her group and happy to know that no harm came to them while she was away, she lets go of Jamie and pokes her head in the tent to see Linc. Stepping in, she takes off her boots and sees him playing with a small toy car that he stuffed in his pocket before they ran out of their house. He looks up at his mom with surprise and gets on his knees as fast as he can. Bending down to grab her son, she pulls him into her chest. *The best feeling in the world is to know that he is safe and warm.* His little arms wrap around his mom, and he lays his head down on her shoulders. Holding him like her little infant, she thinks, *He will always be my baby.* Casey holds Linc tightly, rocking him back and forth; she lets him feel all the comfort and safety she has to offer. For a moment she stays still, and she silently thanks Jesus that they are all safe.

"Mommy, you made it! I thought you weren't coming back." Linc pulls his head back to look at Casey. He moves one of his little arms and places his hand on her forehead, moving her bangs so he can really see her. She looks deep into his troubled eyes and knows that he means it. He really thought that they would not be together again. This troubles Casey, and tears pool in her eyes, knowing he is thinking this because he has not seen Devon. *He thinks that Dad is not coming back, and now he thought I wasn't either. What a sad, brave little boy, dealing with so much heartache and so many problems.* She sucks her tears back and tries to sound brave also.

"I will always come back to you, son. You are my world, and I will do anything and everything that I can for you." She breathes in deeply for a second while she watches her boy. After a few seconds Casey says, smiling, "Guess what I got for you."

She puts Linc and her bag down to look for the meat.

"What is it? What do you got?" Linc questions, with such excitement he starts leaning toward his mom's backpack trying to see what surprise she has in store for him.

Pulling out the grocery bag, she opens it so he can see. Jamie steps in the tent and settles down next to him. The dogs follow behind and lie down at the foot of the sleeping bag. Watching everybody settle down, she thinks, *What a great feeling of accomplishment! We did something right, and now we get to reap the benefits of killing the mountain lion.* Grinning, she gives a piece of meat to everyone. Even the dogs get a piece; after all, they helped kill the cat.

Looking at everybody, and before they take a bite, she prays out loud, "Thank you, Jesus, for this blessing. In Jesus's name… Amen."

The dogs devoured their meat before the prayer was done. Casey watches her son and Jamie close their eyes and sink their teeth into their first bite of the meat. She hears her friend moan with how good it is. Lincoln has a grin on his face as he enjoys filling his belly. Finally, Casey sinks her teeth into the meat, taking a big bite. *It is so delicious! After a week of canned food, fresh meat is amazing.* They are quiet as they enjoy the savory blessing from God. She wants to eat it fast, but she keeps telling herself to take her time and enjoy this moment of victory. Once they are all done, they settle down to sleep.

"Thank you, Jesus, for your blessing to help us continue to survive." Casey closes her eyes and, with a full stomach, easily drifts off into sleep.

Chapter 8

asey awakes the next morning feeling refreshed from a full belly and finally some good rest. Waking up without stomach pain makes her smile. *We can get some miles behind us today. What a little bit of food can do to jump-start our morale.* Getting up earlier than the rest, she gets dressed, planning to hunt just in case they can add to their food supply. Unzipping the tent, she looks outside and sees big snowflakes falling form the sky. Her heart sinks. *No! Why?* Casey wanted to get a good walk in today, but the weather has other ideas. At least a foot of snow has already fallen, and it is still coming down. The wind howls in her ears as it blows and whips the snow around everywhere. *This is just great. We have perfect conditions for a blizzard,* Casey thinks. Zipping up the tent, she thinks for a minute on what they are going to do.

"What's wrong?" Jamie asks as she is waking up out of her slumber.

"I think a blizzard is coming."

"Really? What are we going to do?" she asks, concerned.

"I am going to get out there and try to set our traps, and then I plan to cut down some branches to put over our tent for extra protection and support. We are going to have to stay put until the storm passes, and hopefully it won't last long, because I do not know if we can make it through this."

"Do you want me to start cutting down the branches?" Jamie asks, trying to make the best of this situation.

"I just don't want you or Linc to get sick. We do not have much for fevers or flu," Casey says.

She empties her son's bag so she can add a few items that she feels are important, and then kisses his forehead since he is still dreaming. He looks so precious while he is away in dreamland, and she hopes he sleeps in so the time passes more quickly.

Stepping out of the tent, she lets Komodo follow her into the blizzard. She looks back at Jamie. "Please do not go far from the tent, and make sure you keep it in view if you do step out. If you just want to sit in here and play with Linc, it will not hurt my feelings. I would rather you guys stay safe."

Jamie nods her head with a small smile. Casey can tell she did not want her to go. Zipping up the tent after stepping out, she leaves her friend, child, and Baby Girl behind. The storm is picking up, with snowflakes falling faster and wind whipping them around everywhere. Her nose and eyes sting from the bite of the cold. It is like God has tipped over his bucket of snow and turned on his fan to blow it around. The visibility is not good; she can only see about ten feet in front of her, so she better not go too far; she is afraid she might get lost wandering around in this weather. *When I was sitting at my kitchen table back at home and I thought about coming out in the woods, this was one of my fears. How are we supposed to survive this? The only hope I have is that the storm does not last long. The storms in South Dakota normally come and go pretty fast, but that does not mean this one will.* After walking a while in the blizzard with the wind slapping her with snow, she can really feel the cold settle in her bones. Finally they make it to the creek, where she is even more careful to watch her steps since the snow layer is getting thicker. She does not want to step in a hole or into the water. It would be really bad to break an ankle out here. At last finding a spot that she thinks will be a good place for the traps, she kneels down in the snow and sets them, doubting she will get anything in this kind of weather, but she has already decided to at least try for her son. Not too far away there is a tree that looks easy to climb.

The wind has picked up, and it is hard to see more than a few feet in front of her. Komodo blends in perfectly, lying in the snow bank. *He is meant for this kind of weather,* she thinks and smiles as she watches him wiggle his nose in the snow. Sitting and shivering in the tree for a while, she decides that it is getting too dangerous to be out here alone. Afraid that she is not going to find her way back, Casey climbs down the tree, and they walk back toward the camp.

Finally getting through the maze of the blizzard, she sees that Jamie was able to cut down some pine branches and has placed them on top of the tent. The pine needles catch the snow, perfectly creating a winter roof. Stepping inside, she finds her friend and Linc playing Go Fish with a deck of cards. Their legs are under the sleeping bag for warmth, and Casey takes her boots off to slip under it with them. She adjusts herself so Baby Girl can curl up on her lap. Her pit licks Casey's hand and moves so she can pet her head.

They spend the next three days stuck in the tent playing card games and eating their meat while trying to stay warm. The tent is small, and they take turns to stand and stretch. Casey periodically gets out of the tent to let the dogs go to the bathroom and check on the weather. She hasn't been able to check the traps because of the visibility, and although the snow has stopped, the wind is too much to bear.

On the fourth day of the blizzard the visibility is still terrible, and the wind stings her face as she lets the dogs out. It is still hard to see past a few feet. Casey shivers while trying to stretch her legs, watching Komodo hop around in the snow like a huge bunny, enjoying the weather. Baby Girl just sits next to her owner's feet, shivering, ready to go back in the tent. Once she steps back inside the dogs follow, and she settles down. Her pit curls up in her lap to try to warm up.

Casey pulls out their food to see what they have left. Looking at the meat, she can see that in a few days it will all be gone. Hoping that they would be moving by now and that the meat would hold them over, this storm has put them right back in the same position they were in before it hit. *So much for feeling good about getting this meat.*

Watching Linc and Jamie playing cards, she smiles weakly, thinking, *If we hadn't had the meat before this storm came through, we would be starving right now. However, we will be down to a few cans of food in a few days and will be hungry all over again.* Hearing Lincoln cough, which he has been doing for most of the day, she worries that he is getting sick. Placing her hand on his forehead, she checks to see if he is running a fever.

"I'm fine, Mom!" Linc says, annoyed.

"I am just checking, son," she says after feeling his head. He still feels the same; he is not running any fever, and he shows a lot of energy. *Hopefully it is just a cold that will pass. If the wind would just stop we could keep going. Maybe tomorrow will be better.*

The next day Casey wakes up early and, not hearing the wind howling, gets up to put on her layers of clothing. Stepping outside, she sees that the sun is shining and the snow is still like a blanket covering the ground. The snow crystals reflect the sun, blinding her and forcing her to look the other way. The sky has no clouds in sight, and she believes the storm has passed so they can keep going. She is eager to get moving since they have been stuck in the tent for so many days. Lucky to be alive after surviving the blizzard, she's even more determined to make it to their cabin. *If we can make it through the rampage in town and a blizzard out of town, then we can make it through anything.*

Chapter 9

"Lincoln, Jamie, get up. We have a nice day," Casey calls through the tent door, while her dogs push to get out and move around for the day. Komodo is like a kid in a candy store, hopping through the snow and burying his nose in it. She smiles while watching her big dog play like a kid, hopping around and running as fast as he can, back and forth, in front of the tent. They had many days of rest, which rejuvenated her; and with a new burst of energy, she is ready to conquer the woods. Linc, fully dressed, steps out of the tent, squinting his eyes from the bright sun reflecting off the snow.

"It is so bright out here, Mom!" He tries to cover his eyes with his hands.

Jamie steps out next with her bag and pulls out the meat to split among them and even gives some to their dogs to keep them happy. Smiling, Casey thinks they all look better and ready to move on. Everybody seems relieved to step out into the rays of sun.

"We don't have much food left," Jamie says, putting the food back in her bag before she zips it up.

"I know. I will have to go check on the traps and bring them back before we take off today," Casey responds, but she is not ready to be sad about their situation. "Son, can you come here?" His eyes finally adjust to the light, and he walks over to his mother, who gives him a big hug as she looks into his face. His big brown eyes are twinkling with happiness as he watches Komodo rolling in the snow behind her.

"Linc, we have a big day of walking, so make sure you help Jamie while I'm gone. I have to go get the traps, but I will be back as soon as I can."

"I know, Mom. I'll help Jamie." Then he looks down at the ground and brushes the top of the snow with his boot. Casey hears him cough a few times and narrows her eyes in concern, uncertain how much longer he can be out here. She gives him a hug and sighs, knowing she cannot do anything to change that he is getting sick.

"Komodo, come on, boy," she calls after her excited puppy as she looks away and heads toward their traps, leaving the others behind. He runs to catch up, ready for the next adventure. They make their way down to the creek, stepping through the blanket of snow. As expected, her steps are not deep because they did not have a lot of snowfall, just a lot of wind that made the blizzard conditions. Thankfully it will be easier for today's journey; plus it will melt faster. Unfortunately, nothing was caught in the traps, so Casey pulls them up and straps them to her bag. After smashing a hole in the ice with her boot, she pulls out her water bottles and refills them. Looking across the creek, she freezes as she spots a fresh footprint in the snow. Staying as still as she can, with shivers running through her body, she strains to listen, stretching her ears as far as they can go, but she does not hear anything. Expecting to see someone, she looks all around the woods but sees nothing. Taking a closer look at the footprints, she notices they are all on the other side and trail off into the woods away from the creek. *We are not alone! We need to get out of here!* Placing her water back in her bag and pulling out her gun for safety, she darts her eyes around in the woods to see if she spots somebody, anybody.

Komodo curiously watches with his head cocked to the side and circles Casey, sensing how tense she is. Backing up slowly, she keeps staring at the other side of the creek just in case someone comes out. Her dog quietly follows her, scanning the woods as well. His hair stands on end, knowing that she's not comfortable with the situation. Now hidden behind the trees, she looks back, scanning every inch of the woods, thinking somebody may be watching her. Once they are far enough away, she runs back to camp, moving fast through the trees. Komodo keeps up, giving a low growl, sensing her fear.

Maybe this person came to the creek earlier and did not see my traps and just left. Maybe they are another person who ran away just in time, like us, or they are the military guys who are looking for people. Either way, I am scared now. They have been in the woods for a few weeks and have had no human contact. She doesn't know how bad it is in town or if other people are in the woods. Being women and a kid makes them easy targets. And she thinks again, *We have to get out of here!*

Casey races back to Linc and Jamie as fast as she can, with Komodo right behind her. She worries that somebody may have found them. *What if they are being attacked right now and I cannot do anything for them? If anything happens to my son, I will never forgive myself!*

Moving quickly through the woods, she stumbles, and before she knows what is going on her foot gets caught under a tree root hidden in the snow and she falls onto the ice-cold ground. Her knees hit hard, and she feels sharp pains shooting up her legs, but her quick hands catch the ground before her face smacks it. Letting out a small cry, she sees the snow blowing away from the ground next to her face. Casey, adrenaline pumping, picks herself up quickly to look around and see if anybody is coming. Seeing no one, she brushes off the snow and takes a step forward. A small but sharp pain comes from her knee as she takes a few steps forward, reminding her to slow down. *I have to calm down.* She moves forward again, trying to get back to her family, but Casey's knee prevents her from running. Walking at a fast pace with a limp, she pushes through the pain to get back to the camp.

Finally, she sees the clearing where the others are waiting for her as they finish rolling up the tent. Smiling in relief that they are OK and nothing has happened to them, Casey grabs Linc to give him a hug now that she sees he is safe.

"See, Mom, I helped Jamie pack everything up," he explains, coughing.

"Good job! Mom is very proud of your hard work. Way to go, little buddy," she replies as she pulls away from him.

Looking at Jamie, she says, "Someone else is close by us," and explains what she saw at the creek.

Jamie, concerned and seeing her friend hiding a limp, asks, "Are you OK?"

Unwilling to admit that she panicked out there, that her brain spins in hyperactive mode when she is scared, and knowing she is supposed to be the rock of the group, she cannot let her son see her out of control. "I'm fine. Let's just get going," Casey responds, and helps Jamie finish the last of the packing.

Chapter 10

Finally, the group is on the move again, back on course to the lake, still following the creek upstream but hiding in the forest just out of sight in case someone is following them. The blizzard has slowed them down, but they keep pushing forward. With every step through the hills, Casey's mind is on high alert. Her eyes dart through the trees looking for possible danger. Step by step, they drag their feet through the melting slushy snow. Casey has a slight limp that she pretends is not hurting. Checking her leg about halfway through the day, she sees that it is swollen, with dried blood on the kneecap. Lincoln continues to move despite his cough and runny nose. His cheeks are red, and his mom keeps checking for a fever. Luckily, there is no high temperature yet, and they keep moving. The faster they can get to the cabin, the better.

Each day that goes by, the group grows hungrier and slower. A few days after the blizzard they ate the last of the meat and are now down to eating one can of food a day. Water is the only thing that makes their stomachs think they are full. By the fourth day after the blizzard they move like turtles all over again with no energy. Every morning Casey gets up early to hunt, and with no success, she has decided that she is a terrible hunter. All of them have lost so much weight from the minimal food supplies. Even the dogs are so thin she can see every rib on their sides. Lincoln now coughs all the time and hacks up mucus every few feet. She is scared for the future and wonders how they are going to make it. The only thing they have is the dream that if they can make it to the cabin, things will get better, and Casey keeps reminding her son to keep him going. As the days go on, he fights with his mom, wanting to go home and see his dad. Keeping him from giving up uses so much of her energy.

The weather continues to warm up, the snow melts, and the sun is higher in the sky. Casey knows they should reach the lake soon. They have no other choice. According to the map, once they are at the lake they need to walk around to the other side and follow a road that will bring them to the dirt road that goes directly to the town of Rochford. Their cabin is not too far outside of this small town.

She wakes up on the seventh day bright and early in the morning and leaves to hunt. Going down by the creek, trying to be very aware of the surroundings, she is still worried about the footsteps that she saw a few days back. She sits in a tree for a while scouting for something to eat, thinking one of these days a deer will come along and she can kill it. Komodo, who has been deemed her hunting partner, is lying down below the tree. Having been in the woods for a few weeks, she still has not even had a chance to actually kill anything except the mountain lion. Also, she has not even had a bite from her animal traps. She does not know what she's doing wrong, which just saddens her heart.

After about an hour she hears a noise across the creek. She perks her ears up, and so does Komodo. Still thinking it may be a person, she sits very still and finally sees a deer slowly creep up to the creek. It is a beautiful light-tan doe with white fur on its belly that follows all the way to the tail. The deer's ears twitch in every direction, listening to the sounds of the forest. Stepping slowing to the creek, it lowers it head to take a drink. Her body is perfectly placed, only twenty feet away from where Casey has a clear shot to its heart. Finally, she has a chance to shoot. The deer is in her sights, and taking a deep breath, she grabs her bow, draws back the arrow and releases it. The deer senses danger, and her immediate reaction is to bend her knees while lowering her head. Casey's arrow sweeps past the deer just above her back and drives into the dirt. The animal's ears twitch again, and her head cocks back quickly to see what is going on. With just a small hesitation, the deer darts as fast as it can away from the creek and back into the trees for safety. Casey lost her chance, thinking, *For the first time since we have been out in the woods I had a chance and I blew it.* Still in the same stance, she finally lowers her bow as deep sadness sweeps all over her. For an uncertain amount of time, she stares at the neon-pink feather of her arrow sticking out of the ground, knowing she has no one to blame but herself for losing that deer.

Finally mustering up her strength, she climbs down, where Komodo nudges her hand to pet him. "I messed it up, boy. It is my fault." He tries to give her some comfort while she thinks that if he had barked, she could blame it on him, but he hadn't. Her dog did what he was supposed to do: he stayed quiet and watched. She gives him a last pet and steps next to the small creek to see where to cross to retrieve her arrow. Finding some rocks, she crosses and yanks the arrow out of the ground. Looking back, her dog is now sniffing the water, deciding if he wants a drink. Casey knows he is hungry, just as hungry as they are. Crossing back over the creek, they make their way back to camp with very heavy, slow, depressing steps, her head hanging low as they are coming back with no food again.

Once they reach camp she can see Jamie and Linc have already packed everything and are sitting on some rocks sharing a can of peaches. Casey sits down next to them and waits for them to finish eating, feeling worse knowing that was the last can of food. God gave her a chance, and she blew it. *We need to make it at least another week, and I do not know how we are going to do it.*

"Do you want some?" Jamie asks, directing the can of peaches to her.

She shakes her head no and pets Baby Girl, who came over to greet her. The dogs are so skinny compared to when they started. How these animals have stayed by her side through all of this is beyond her. *They should have left us behind and started hunting on their own. I do not want to shoot and eat them.* She knows people have done such things, or even worse, in the past to survive. *How long will we go before we contemplate this kind of idea?* she wonders.

"Are we ready?" Jamie asks with enthusiasm.

"I am. Are you, Mom?" Linc asks.

She gives a weak smile, swallows her sadness, and nods her head yes. Then she stands with the rest of the group, and they get moving.

They spend the day climbing a hill that never seems to end. The weather has warmed up, and it may be around forty degrees. The sun is shining through the trees, giving them a burst of rays, as they march to their destination. The birds are out tweeting to their own melodies. The sound from the creek creates a rhythm with the birds' melodies and the breeze that makes its own sway of a tune, all perfectly aligned together. The peace of the forest mixed with the melody and rhythm helps to steady Casey's grumbling stomach. The tunes help her to concentrate on moving forward one step at a time. She would rather focus on the sounds of the forest than the noise in her head. The constant stress of survival for her child has drained her. *Was coming out in the woods a good choice? Did I only prolong my existence for a few more weeks? Who really knows the answer to these questions? What I do know is that we are here, we are alive and moving. The animals have adapted to the forest to survive day in and day out. They have officially conformed to the woods for their needs.* This is never what Casey wanted for them, and she thinks, *I just didn't know what else to do. I must focus back to the march of our steps, the tweet of the birds, and the sounds of the wind rustling, with the rush of the stream.* They continue to march to the rhythm of the woods they have come to know.

It must be in the afternoon sometime, and they can finally see the top of the hill they've been gradually climbing all day. Slowly, they take each step since the end of this hill has steepened. Linc is right in front of Casey, and her hands are ready to catch him if he slips. After several minutes of fighting to the top of the hill they finally make it and are relieved to see Sheridan Lake.

With a heavy sigh, Casey says, "We made it."

"This looks like a great place to stop for the day," Jamie says.

Looking around the beautiful lake that is hidden in the hills, Casey nods her head in agreement. Originally, it was formed from a manmade dam that was created to control the water coming into town. During the summertime it is filled with fishing boats and people who love to camp and swim, and in the winter people come out to ice fish. They search until they find a small hiding place on the other side of a hill away from the lake.

"Son, would you like to go down to the lake with me and try to catch some fish?"

"I guess if I have to," he states reluctantly as he gets up to leave with his mom.

She pulls out a small collapsible fishing pole that is in her bag, and they, with Komodo, walk down to the lake to drop the hook in the water. *It is nice to relax a little earlier than normal,* she thinks and hopes that hunting by the lake will give her better luck. Linc seems to enjoy relaxing by the water, and since the ice is mostly melted, he watches it move freely.

"Are we ever going to see Daddy again?" he asks in a very serious tone, unable to look at her.

Such a young child has matured so much in the last couple of weeks. He is a lot quieter these days, lost in his own thoughts. No more does he asks for pizza or to watch TV. He follows directions clearly and effectively. The struggle has hardened him. When he falls he does not ask for help and gets up pretending that nothing has happened. His innocence and carefree life flew from his eyes the day they left the grocery store. He clearly understands the world is not safe nor does it care if he survives.

"I don't know, son. I hope one day we will see him again," Casey says very methodically.

"I'm mad at you for leaving him. It is your fault Daddy is not here, and I will never forgive you," he spits out angrily. This is the first time she has heard him talk to her so spitefully, yet she understands it all, every piece of built-up resentment that he has been harvesting and growing since they left.

Casey chokes tears and tries to control her shaky voice as she says, "I know you're angry, and if we could have waited, I would have. I miss Dad too."

"I'm done. I want to see Jamie now." His eyes are narrowed into two small, dark daggers.

He stands up and runs back to the tent, leaving his mom and Komodo behind. She sits there in sadness staring at the water. Her heart feels like a ton of bricks that weigh down her body. The tears stream freely from her eyes. There is nothing she can do to heal her son's broken heart. *I am the cause of his anger. I am the one who dragged him out here. Though I did not cause our town to get attacked, I did make the decision to come out in the woods. If there was a definition of a hero, I would not be it. I do not know if I even qualify for survival.*

Komodo feels Casey's sadness and sits down in front of her, looking into her face. She smiles weakly at this beautiful dog that follows her everywhere she goes. He inches his nose slowly to her face; then he lowers his head under her chin. She grabs his fur and pulls him in for a hug. Holding on to his fur tightly, she pets the side of his body, with her face tucked into his neck. She clings to the comfort from her dog, who is the only one who sees that she is trying. He is the only one who sees her pain.

The sun starts to set, and Casey decides to return to camp. Walking up to the tent, she overhears Lincoln say to Jamie, "I just don't understand why we had to leave my dad. Why does she get to decide what is best for us? You should decide what is best for the group."

"Linc, your mom is trying to keep us safe. Remember, the tanks and buses came to your house and we didn't have a choice; we had to leave." Jamie tries to justify his mom's actions.

"Whatever. I still think you should lead the group," he says to end the conversation.

Casey takes a deep breath to control her emotions, now knowing exactly how her son feels about her. She opens the tent flap and steps inside. Linc and Jamie are playing cards, and Komodo joins Baby Girl, who's curled up in the corner of the tent. At least they have each other, and he can confide in Jamie for comfort. Sitting down next to them, she picks up the Bible to read to herself until it is too dark to see. Her pit gets up and climbs into her lap. Casey gives a small smile and hugs her for comfort. *Maybe tomorrow will be a better day. We just have to keep fighting, and it will get better.*

Chapter 11

The next day Casey gets up early, as usual, to go hunting, still hoping she will get something. She watches Linc, who is asleep, looking so sweet, and kisses him on his forehead, even though his words from yesterday still hurt. They cut deep into her already wounded heart, and her only hope is that once he is older he will understand why she pushed them into the woods.

Komodo follows behind her as they leave the campsite, and they head toward the lake where it spills into a stream. Casey finds a hidden spot in a tree and perches herself in it. The morning is cool but without a cloud in sight, and she is sure it's going to be a nice day. Leaning her back against the trunk of the tree, she closes her eyes, thinking, *I could sit in the forest resting all day.* Her Pyrenees steps over to the flowing liquid and takes a drink of water before he makes his way to the tree that she is in, circles in front of it, and finds a comfortable place to lie down. For some time they listen to the birds and enjoying the rhythm of the woods. Then she finally sees a deer in the distance, steadily walking to the creek to quench its thirst.

Her bow ready to shoot, she leans forward and pulls back the arrow. The deer is about fifteen feet away, and she follows it, keeping the animal in her sights, aiming for its heart. Watching the deer, she sees it twitch its ears listening to all the sounds of the woods as it slowly makes its way to the water. Trying to stay still and quiet, Casey's heart is beating rapidly with anticipation to have another chance to feed her family. She takes a steady breath as the feather of the arrow brushes her cheek before she lets it go. It zips through the trees, past the creek, right into the side of the buck. The animal jumps in pain and tries to hop away from the stream. It stumbles to the ground and kicks it legs until it cannot struggle anymore.

I got him, she thinks, which lifts her spirits a little, though she can still feel the weight of her stress. She climbs down the tree and watches Komodo run ahead of her. He circles and sniffs the deer, but Casey holds back a few minutes to make sure it is dead, not wanting to be kicked. The animal moves its head around, watching her dog pace by, and tries to swing his antlers, still putting up a fight. Komodo jumps back, not feeling the need to attack, knowing this animal is too weak. Once the buck finally closes its eyes and stops breathing, Casey steps over to it and pulls her arrow out of the deer. Looking at this creature, she places her hand on its fur and appreciates the life that she took to feed her family, and she thinks, *Thank God for this food.*

Smiling to herself, she feels a little bit of pride knowing she finally did it and got some food for her family. Her dog steps up next to his owner, nudging her for some attention, and she pets the top of his head. Then she starts the process to field dress the buck, which lightens her spirits even more while she builds a fire pit to cook their meat. *We have food again! What a better way to start the day.* After skinning it she gets the fire started to cook the meat. She tries to move fast, quickly cutting the flesh, so she can get back to the group to show them some success. After working hard for a few hours until it's all cooked, Casey cleans her knives and wraps up the meat to take back to camp. *Finally, I am able to successfully hunt a deer,* she thinks. This should help sustain them for the rest of the trip. She is so excited to get back to share this news and rushes through the woods. Feeling her happiness, Komodo wags his tail, trailing behind his owner. Once she sees the tent through the trees in the clearing, she grins from ear to ear, knowing that she's almost there. She can finally see Jamie and Linc, but somebody else is with them!

Stopping in her tracks, she steps behind a tree about thirty feet away and glances at her dog with a warning eye that keeps him from barking, but he is growling under his breath as he hears Baby Girl barking like crazy. She puts her bag down behind the tree and grabs her gun. Cocking it, she creeps behind one tree after another to get closer to camp, with her dog following each of her steps. Once in earshot, she stops and hides behind the trunk of a big pine tree; then she points to the ground to tell her dog to lie down. It is taking everything he has to listen to his owner, growling quietly with his hair standing straight up. The more he hears her pit, the shakier he gets.

"Don't you let that dog go, or I will shoot you!" yells an ugly man, who has obviously been out in the woods as long as they have.

He has dark, curly hair that is grown out and has not been brushed in a while, with a thick, wavy beard, and he is wearing a lightweight coat that looks like it has been torn by tree branches while running through the forest. His jeans are dirty, with holes in the knees, and his hiking boots are untied and muddy. Looking very worn down and manic, he must be hungry and willing to do what he has to, to get what he needs.

"I won't. Just—just don't shoot us. Take whatever you need," Jamie says as calmly as she can.

Slowly she pushes Linc behind her, taking one calm step at a time away from the tent for protection while staying slightly bent over, holding on to Baby Girl's harness as tightly as she can. The pit is growling and barking viciously, ready to protect her family. Her barks are loud and strong enough to muffle the sounds of Casey's footsteps as she slowly and lightly steps toward her group. Jamie can clearly see her and continues to move away from the supplies, trying to keep the man's attention on her. Linc makes eyes contact with his mom, and when she is about ten feet away from the man she puffs out her chest and raises her gun at this hateful person.

"I want all of your food and weapons… NOW!" he yells at her family.

He hollers at my loved ones, who are the only reason I am out here in these hills. They are the only reason I try to keep going. Casey narrows her eyes hatefully as she aims her gun to his back.

"No one yells at my family," she whispers.

Harnessing all of her anger from the current event that has engulfed their lives, now she has to face this man who thinks he can take from them, too. *No, he will not take from us!* she thinks before her mind goes blank. Never taking her eyes off of him, she slowly squeezes the trigger. The bullet propels forward, hitting the guy in his back, and flies through his body and out of his chest. He never saw her coming because of Baby Girl's loud barks. Once the gun goes off Jamie turns her body and falls on top of Linc, pushing him to the ground while the bullet darts above them. As she falls she releases their pit, who lurches forward, waiting for her chance to get this man who slams to the ground at the same time. As he falls he lets go of his gun, dropping it in front of him. Their pit jumps between him and the gun, going for his arm and sinking her teeth into him. Casey's dog forgets his owner's orders and rushes over to help his friend.

"Baby Girl, Komodo," she yells at her dogs. They both stop biting but still stay close to the guy on the ground. She steps over the man and kicks the gun away from his reach while watching him struggle to breathe. He slowly pushes himself onto his back and rolls to his side, then looks up at her in fear. *He must have some internal bleeding,* she thinks, watching blood drip from his mouth, and looks at the bullet hole where it exited out of his chest. But she has no sympathy for this man. With her rage in full gear, all she can think is that this man thought he could hurt them. She may not be able to control what is happening in her world, but she can keep this man from hurting them. He will never have a chance again.

"No one threatens my family," she states, with her breathing in complete control and the adrenaline still running through her veins. He starts to cough as he is now choking on his own blood.

"But I will not make you suffer," she says.

Picking up her pistol again, she cocks it and aims straight for his head. He stares at her but does not say anything. He takes one last breath and coughs, trying to brace for the end. Gazing at him, they make eye contact, and Casey never stops staring and takes a deep breath as she compresses the trigger again. The bullet penetrates his head with no mercy.

Once he stops moving and she knows he is dead, bending over, she grabs his gun and his knife attached to his belt. She looks again at the man, who is now frozen in place with blood dripping from the new wound and open eyes that peer back at her. Lifting her hand, she closes his eyes to put him to rest.

Jamie walks over to her friend and puts her hands on her shoulders. "Come on, we have to go. He may not be alone," she whispers very calmly, trying not to scare Linc.

Casey looks up at her with tears welling up in her eyes.

"I know, I know," Jamie says quietly. She lightly pulls on her friend's shoulders to guide her to stand up. "Don't do it, not now. Be strong for your son," she whispers in Casey's ear.

Turning her body, she looks at Linc. His eyes are huge, with tears quietly streaming down his check. He is frozen, petrified, after witnessing his mom kill a man right in front of him. Her brain clicks, and she blinks several times; then she tightens her body, sucking up her tears. Swallowing her pain down her throat and into her stomach, she takes slow steps over to her son, still shaking from the adrenalin that is racing through her. Closing her eyes, she breathes deeply and lifts her jittery hand, grabbing the back of his head, pulling him into a hug.

"It's-it's OK, son. M-M-Mom's here, and I always will be."

He grabs onto her leg as tightly as he can, burying his face to hide his tears. Jamie, as strong as she is, starts packing up as fast as she can. She moves like lightning, racing for dear life, as Casey just stares at the dead man. Finally, she looks down at her son, realizing she needs to help and they need to get out of here.

"Son, we are strong, right? We have to help our friend; we have to leave now," she explains.

Linc nods his head and sits down, too tired to help. Komodo comes over to him, sniffing him to make sure he is OK. Once he is satisfied he sits next to him and watches the women work. Baby Girl lies down between the dead man and Linc, keeping an eye on him like he is going to jump back up and attack them all. She is not going to let this happen. Casey moves her heavy muscles to help Jamie pack their stuff. Trying not to think of the psychological damage she has created for herself and her son, she pushes herself to help where she can, but all she can think is: *What did I do? May God have mercy on my soul!*

Chapter 12

Since Casey just killed a man, she never got a chance to tell her group about the deer. Once packed, and grabbing the bag she left behind the tree, they move out as fast as they can, afraid that there may be more people in the woods. A light jog around the lake brings them to the main road that runs through the hills. She knows this will lead them to the dirt road that will take them to Rochford. Luckily, they refilled their water bottles last night, because they are not near a water source anymore.

Once they can see the main road they stop to catch their breath and think. Casey keeps her eyes on the pavement to see if anybody is coming. They stay back in the trees far enough to not be seen, and she peeks around the tree trunks while they decide the best time to cross. It is pretty quiet for a few minutes as they take a drink, and then far to the right, Casey watches some army vehicles coming toward them. They stay behind the trees and watch while the automobiles drive by. Holding her breath, she hopes no one can see her group. There are six of the army cars and a couple more buses that are trailing behind them, full of people. *What are they doing with the masses?* she keeps thinking, watching them pass by, waiting until the enemy is completely out of their sight and the road is silent again.

"This is it. Let's go—hurry! Casey hollers and grabs Linc's hand.

They scurry across the road and into the forest on the other side, trying not to be seen. It only takes them a few seconds to do what seems like such a life-threatening act. Once they get across and are well hidden from the road, Casey stops dragging her son and they pause to catch their breath for a few seconds. She feels like they are running from one danger to another, yet not sure if they were ever really safe.

"Are you ready?" Jamie asks as she lets out a deep breath, still trying to control her lungs.

"Yeah," Casey says after taking another drink of water.

The fear of that man's having companions is still on their minds, and they need as much distance from that horror as they can. With no time to process their grief, they move more fiercely along the side of the road, just far enough to be hidden out of sight. On high alert of what is going on around them, they are all lost in their own thoughts with not much to say. The dogs stay with the group the entire time and seem to understand the need to be quiet. Every mile behind them brings them even closer to Rochford. Groups of military vehicles and buses periodically drive by, so they continue to hide. Even though Casey believes they are far enough from the road not to be seen, the fear is instilled in them. *The enemy is clearing all of the people out the hills. I just hope the decision to go to Rochford is the right choice,* she thinks as they continue to walk as far as they can until it gets darker. Looking into the horizon, she can feel the weather getting cooler. The sun is settling in for the night, and the stars twinkle across the velvet black sky.

"This spot is as good as any to stop for the night," she says to everybody while she takes her pack off.

They set up camp and by the time they finish it is completely dark. Casey sits down outside of the tent on the ground and says, "Lincoln, Jamie, come here, sit with me, please."

They both slowly take a seat on the ground, looking tired and pretty sad from today's events. Feeling the weight of stress in her muscles, she attempts to sound excited. "I forgot to tell you earlier because of what happened…" she trails off for a second, thinking about being a killer, then looks at her son and comes back to reality. "But this morning when I went hunting, I took so much longer because I got a deer!"

Both Jamie's and Linc's eyes light up as they look at their leader. She reaches into her bag and pulls out some wrapped up meat that she hands out to the group, including the dogs to make sure they are happy as well. Lastly, she gives some to herself. Her group sits in silence as they stuff their mouths with food, enjoying the divine taste of the deer. The dogs wag their tails in enjoyment as they engulf the food.

Once Linc is done he gets up and goes into the tent to lie down. Still not talking to his mom, now she believes he is probably scared of her. *Who knows what is running through the poor kids head?* she thinks, looking down to the ground, knowing there is nothing she can do to change what is happening to him. She picks up some twigs and breaks them, lost in thought.

"Are you OK?" Jamie asks her.

Without looking at her, she says, "I killed a man today. How do you think I am?" She looks squarely into Jamie's eyes to try to read her thoughts, then glances at the ground again, ashamed of herself, not yet fully processing what happened earlier.

"He pointed a gun at your son. He threatened Lincoln's life. That is what you think, that is what keeps you going. No one goes after your son; you keep telling yourself that when you start feeling bad. Everything you are doing is for that boy. This is why we are in the woods right now. This is why you shot this man and any other that may come for your son's life. This is what you tell yourself every day. And, Casey, I would have done the same thing," Jamie says. Then, getting up, she looks down at her friend one more time, seeing Casey stare into nothingness, still breaking more twigs. She places her hand on her friend's shoulder. "I'm with you; don't give up yet. Plus, I think it is Christmas so… Merry Christmas," she says and then steps into the tent to lie down with Linc.

Komodo is lying at Casey's feet, and Baby Girl walks over to her trying to get in her lap. She hugs her pit tightly to feel some comfort and love while she thinks, *Is it really Christmas? What is the date? How long have we been in the woods? Yes, it is probably around Christmas time, and I killed somebody on Jesus's birthday. So much for that.* And she whispers Merry Christmas to herself as tears stream down her face.

By the time Casey goes into the tent Lincoln is already asleep, worn out from today's event. She gets in the sleeping bag next to him and kisses his head before she turns her back to him, ashamed of herself, and closes her eyes to sleep. Eventually she drifts off into a slumber once her mind winds down. Her last thoughts are: *Will God forgive me for my sins?*

Waking up the next day to the rays of the sun absorbing through the tent walls, Casey opens her eyes, which feel like they are burning from the bright light, even though they are probably stinging from waking up so many times to sounds she heard in the forest. Still thinking people are looking for them and concerned the man wasn't alone, she decides not to hunt today because they need to keep going to get more distance between them and the shooting from yesterday.

"Linc, Jamie, let's get up and get going. We can eat on the way. Come on, let's get out of here," she says quietly.

Jamie opens her eyes and starts to stretch her arms. "What's wrong?"

"Nothing. I am just panicking and want to get moving."

"Alright, let's get up and go."

Lincoln rubs his sleepy eyes while listening to them talk and says after a minute, "Why are you panicking, Mom?"

"No reason, son. I am just eager to get out of here and keep going. We have meat, so we do not need to hunt today."

They all three get dressed and step out of the tent. The dogs follow the group out to stretch and move around. *I swear, the weather is getting warmer every day,* she thinks. The scent of fresh pine with a slight morning dew enters her nostrils as she takes a deep breath, ready to start a new day. They pack up fast and head out, while Jamie hands out some meat to everyone as they make their way to Rochford. The further away from the shooting, the better Casey feels, knowing they are close to their final destination and a place for protection so they can finally figure out what to do. Her not hunting gives them more time to put some miles behind them. The military vehicles continue to drive by in both directions. One set of vehicles heads further out of town with empty buses, and other buses head into town full of people. They all know to stop and hide every time they hear the roar of engines disturb the sounds of the forest. After spending so much time in the woods they have learned to hear nature, listening to the birds, wind, and the streams. But when the birds stop singing they know something is bothering the peace. They watch silently to see something new or interesting that is going on. This is how the group knows to stop and listen too.

It takes most of the morning before the group sees a winding dirt road leading into a canyon. Looking up, Casey sees a green street sign pointing toward Rochford. "Here we go, guys—the last stretch," she says enthusiastically as she smiles back at the group, happy they made it this far. They are going to make it; she can feel it now!

We may be able to make it to the cabin before nightfall, she thinks hopefully. Staying to the edge of the forest just as they did on the main road for safety, they spend the afternoon moving quickly through the canyon, feeling they can push themselves on this last stretch of the journey. *Once we are there they can finally just sit down and rest,* Casey thinks, knowing the underground bunker is stocked with supplies and they have additional resources in the cabin. To rest for one day will be nice.

Just before the sun goes down they finally come to the little town of Rochford. There are only five buildings on the dirt road: a general store, a bar, two restaurants, and a gas station. The buildings are all made out of wood, and a wooden porch walkway connects them all. With just a few houses along the side of the road leading up to the town, Casey has always felt this place looks like it is straight out of a Western movie.

They need to walk around the other side of town; their little cabin is a few miles behind it. As they get closer to town the sound of vehicles echoes through the canyon. Ducking low to the ground, they hide behind some big boulders near the main road. Casey peeks around the rocks once the vehicles pass by to see what the enemy is doing. A few men with guns get out of the vehicles and run into the buildings checking one at a time. They clear out any people they find and push them into the buses. She sees men and women, who are frightened, with their hands up doing what the enemy wants. Once they finish looking through the last building they all step out staring at the one-horse town. One guy comes up to his group with gasoline cans. He hands them to the other men, and they pour it all over the outside of the buildings. Once their cans are empty, another man strikes a match and sets them on fire.

Kneeling behind the rocks, Casey's group sadly watches the buildings go up in flames. The old, dry wood doesn't stand a chance. Enormous clouds of smoke rise up in the air as the buildings burn down. The sun is now completely set, leaving it dark, but the fire lights up the night sky, making it easier to see. They must be done searching for people and are making sure nobody can come back and hide. Leaning against the rock, Casey closes her eyes, taking deep breaths, trying not to lose her temper. She is so tired of running from these evil people who are destroying everything in her life.

"Casey, Casey," Jamie whispers.

Opening her eyes, she looks toward Jamie to see that she is holding Linc's hand and retreating further into the woods.

"Come on, we have to get out of here!" Jamie says harshly, but as quietly as she can.

Komodo is right by her, and Baby Girl is planted next to Casey near the rock. Her pit looks at her like she is waiting for her owner to decide what to do next. Looking at her friend, then at her pit, she uses what strength she still has to turn her head and look one more time at the small town that they spent last summer enjoying. No more restaurants, no more general store—this life is done, and they made sure of it.

Turning back, she rushes over to Jamie with Baby Girl on her heels, not ready to leave her owner behind. Once they retreat into the forest a safe distance, they work their way around the burning town. The group stays quiet, scared they will get caught before they reach the winding road that leads to her cabin. She would tell the group to sleep in the cabin tonight, but with all the commotion going on around them, Casey believes the enemy will be checking the woods. They need to get to the bunker as soon as possible to hide in hopes of surviving this storm.

Chapter 13

They finally step onto the driveway in front of the shotgun-style log cabin that Casey's husband built on their ten-acre lot. Nestled in a thick stand of trees, it has a cute little front porch they walk up to, which has flower pots waiting for someone to place some plants in them, and a row of flower beds that lay in front of the porch, hibernating for the winter. Next to the front door is a wooden sign with a bass fish carved in it, which Casey stares at while she opens the door to step inside.

Last summer feels like a lifetime ago. Linc played in his pool and chased Komodo around while Devon continued to work on the underground bunker. Baby Girl, being a true lizard at heart, had found the most comfortable grassy spot where the direct sunlight would hit her and she could absorb every single ray of light. They loved to spend their summer nights on the front porch counting the stars and listening to the crickets sing their night melodies. Devon and his wife had dreamt about retiring right here in this simple lifestyle, where they could grow old together and know that this is what they could give to their son, great memories for him to pass down to his children when he is ready. It had been a simpler time with so much hope for their family, so much fun and love, that she sees when she looks around this cabin. Now it is all about survival and making it from day to day.

Taking a deep breath, she says, "Listen, guys, we need to grab everything that is important or could be important now and get it into the bunker. I want to clean this house out just in case they come up here looking for us."

Jamie looks at her tiredly and nods her head. They all go through the kitchen cabinets for canned food, plates, knives, and cups and then on into the bedrooms. Casey finds some laundry baskets and starts loading them up with blankets and pillows and the kitchen supplies; then she leads her group to the bunker.

At the back of the property the hill slopes up and then back down again. Nestled in the valley are some bushes and tree branches entangled together on the side of the mountain that hide the door to the bunker, and trees are scattered throughout the property that help to hide their secret place. They go to the side of the hill, and Casey shoves the branches away to reveal a small latch to a wooden door that she pulls open, allowing them to step inside their hideout. It is about the size of average living room, and she walks across it to grab the oil lamp and give them some light. There are four cots on the floor, with two against one wall and two on the other side. The back wall has shelves built against it that are full of canned food, guns, gunpowder, bullets, and other supplies. There is a small table next to the corner of the shelves with two chairs that are next to one of the cots.

Casey remembers setting this place up and thinking how foolish they were to spend so much money on this project. If she had only known then what she knows now, she would have spent more money and time on supplies and resources and would not have picked on her husband for wanting to be so prepared. He is the only reason they have a chance, and he is not even with them.

"Come on, let's get more stuff out of the house," Jamie says and heads out.

"Lincoln, stay here. We will be right back," his mother says.

He nods his head, understanding, and with it being so late at night, she sees how exhausted her son is. He lies down on one of the cots, and she places a blanket on him. Kissing him on his forehead, she whispers, "Good night, sweet boy."

Closing his eyes, he turns away to fall asleep. She hurries out of the bunker to catch up with Jamie. They both have laundry baskets in their hands, and they fill them with anything that seems useful. Casey even grabs some of the board games for Linc and reaches for clothes, jackets, soap, and some paper and pens. Back and forth the girls go, grabbing almost anything. Having spent more than a month with no household supplies, everything seems important. Only those things they can't fit in the baskets stays behind. On her fourth trip she grabs flashlights and tools and hurries through the living room, when she sees out of the corner of her eyes a picture hanging on the wall of her son and his dad. Stopping, she stares at her handsome husband, who is about six feet tall with dark hair and dark-brown eyes. In this picture, he is starting to grow a beard, though he normally has a goatee. He has a small smile. His son's dirty-blond hair, with tips highlighted from the summer sun, is long enough to stick up in the air, which has always been Linc's favorite style. Now his hair has grown past that stage and hangs down over his ears. In the picture Linc's big brown eyes twinkle and he has a grin on his face. He enjoys time with his dad, and it is easy to see in this picture. She grabs the frame from the wall and puts it in the basket, then continues picking up books and everything she can. Jamie is also reaching for whatever she can, and then they finally look around at the ransacked house.

"I guess we can try grabbing more tomorrow. I think we have the most important stuff, plus some extra," Jamie says.

Nodding her head in agreement, Casey feels her adrenaline winding down and exhaustion kicking in. Since seeing the fire, the fear of those men coming up here has kept them moving fast, but now their bodies are telling them that they are done and it is time to go to sleep. They are too tired to fight anymore tonight. Both of the girls head back to the underground bunker with their hands full of stuff.

Once they step into the hidden home Casey puts the laundry basket down on the floor and looks over at Linc, who is sleeping. Baby Girl has curled up on his blanket at the end of the bed, trying to stay warm, while Komodo is lying on the dirt floor in front of her son's cot. Even when the dogs are resting they are in a protective position, never leaving their humans unguarded.

She goes over to the other cot next to her son and places her gun on the table next to her bed. Grabbing one of the blankets and pillows, she lies down as well. Jamie does the same and smiles weakly at her friend before she places her head on the pillow. *What an amazing feeling: to settle my head on this soft pillow,* Casey thinks as her head sinks into this light, fluffy surface that she embraces immediately and falls asleep with her last thoughts: *We did it, we made it to the bunker.*

The next day Casey wakes up hearing Linc laughing. Opening her eyes, she sees her son and friend playing a card game at the kitchen table. Not sure how long she has been sleeping, she sits up and grabs one of the bottles of water to drink. "What time is it?" Casey asks.

"Not sure. I just thought you could use the rest," Jamie explains while she concentrates on her next move in the game.

"Thanks. I appreciate that. Lincoln, how do you feel, buddy?" she asks as she gets up and stretches.

"Fine, Mom," he says sharply, working hard to beat Jamie. Hearing Linc's tone, she hopes it is about the game and not that he is still mad at her.

"If it is OK, I think I am going to step outside to get some fresh air and see what is going on around us. Do either of you want to come?" she asks. Linc does not respond, and Jamie looks at him and then at Casey, shrugging her shoulders and nodding her head sadly.

"Go ahead. We are still playing our game," she offers.

Looking down at the pile of stuff on the ground that they grabbed last night, Casey notices a hand mirror at the top of a pile. She picks it up and looks at her reflection. She sees long, dark hair that is pulled back in a high ponytail. Strands of her hair, which used to be bangs but are now grown out with a natural spiral wave, have fallen to the side of her face. She has highlights that are growing out but can only be seen in her hair when it lies freely. Looking at her face, she can see her high cheek bones and big dark-brown eyes. Her face looks sad and tired, or maybe she just feels sad and tired. All over her face she has smears and smudges of dirt and mud that hide her naturally light-golden-brown skin that tends to easily tan in the sunlight. Either way, her reflection is the image of struggle and hardship. She does not see much beauty here, just someone who is unkempt and dirty because she does not have the time to maintain her self-image.

Putting down the mirror in disgust, she thinks, *I will go down to the stream behind our land and clean my face.* Casey turns back around to look at her group, realizing they are just as dirty as she is. They had been well-kempt people before this attack, but during their time in the woods they never brought up their cleanliness, never wasted water on their faces or washed their clothes. Always on the move to make sure they were not caught, and with no time to take care of themselves, they made it here for protection.

"All right, I will be back in a little bit," Casey says; then she turns around to leave their little bunker.

Once outside she believes that this is one of the nicest days they've had since they started their journey. Komodo is eager to follow his owner and explore this new place. The rays of the sun make her eyes squint after being in the dark bunker. She feels like every cell in her skin is trying to absorb the waves of energy that the sun is willing to give. Taking a deep breath, she smells the scent of pine needles and fresh morning dew, which makes her feel better and recharged for life.

The bunker door is hidden between two sloping hills, giving Casey a little hidden protection when she steps out. Not being able to see the cabin from here is exactly what her husband wanted, to place the bunker in a spot that is not noticeable to anybody else. She decides to head down to the stream at the bottom of the other side of the hill, just outside of their property line. Her land sits against the state forest, which means they have no neighbors near them and they are completely isolated in the woods. She brings her water, gun, and knife, just in case she needs them, as she makes her way to the stream with her dog prancing happily behind her.

Once she is at the creek, Casey gets down on her knees to clean her face. *It feels good to put the cold water to my skin and scrub the dirt and grime off,* she thinks while enjoying the calm day, which is turning out to be pretty nice. The sun is high in the sky and there is a slight breeze. The birds are chirping to their own tune as she watches them dance around in the tree branches. The stream is clear and untouched, rolling nicely down the hill. The grass is dry and warm underneath her as she sits, leaning against a tree trunk. With no rush to get anywhere, Casey sighs with relief and thinks, *Just maybe we will be safe for a moment, just a moment to breathe. Tomorrow we can decide what chores we need to do and how to sustain ourselves, but today we get to relax.* She watches her dog take a drink from the creek; then he wanders by sniffing the tree before he settles down next to her. She scratches him behind his ear as he pants, enjoying the love he is receiving.

"Thank you, Jesus," she says under her breath, appreciating that they finally made it, that they are finally safe.

Leaning against the tree for a while with her eyes closed and soaking in the rays from the sun, she enjoys some peace and quiet. All at once she smells something foul in the air. Casey opens her eyes and takes another breath and can smell something, something that is burning. Looking around, she does not see any present danger, and then she looks up to the sky and sees big, black smoky clouds rolling into the atmosphere. Her dog lifts his head, smelling the air as well, and stands up knowing something is wrong. She gets up quickly, seeing that the clouds are not far from them, and she runs back toward the bunker as fast as she can with her dog pacing behind her, wanting to find out what is going on as they rush toward danger. Once they reach the valley with her bunker she can see that the fire is not on them. Taking a deep breath in relief, she steps toward the hill that blocks them from their cabin. Watching the black smoke rise from the hilltop, she lowers herself to the ground and crawls up to the edge of the hill to peek over it. Komodo follows his owner's lead, getting on his belly as well, and inches his way up with her.

It's her cabin, and she can see men laughing and enjoying themselves as they burn it down! One soldier slaps another other one on his back like he made some great joke. Anger runs through Casey's veins as she narrows her eyes in rage and tightens her muscles, ready to react. It takes everything in her not to shoot them. She wants them to stop laughing at burning down her home that her husband worked hard on and the memories of her life that are going up in smoke! Trying to control her breathing with deep breaths, she continues to focus on this exercise as she chokes down her rage. *If I come up unexpectedly on them I can shoot them all. There are only three of them, and I can take their home and everything that matters to them. Then they will know how it feels to have their world destroyed,* she thinks.

As she gets up to execute her unthought-out plan, she cocks her gun and starts to raise it when Komodo lifts his head, sniffing the air and watching his owner, wanting to help. Just then she hears, "Come on, we have more homes to check. Let's get out of here." Another man hollers as he comes from around the other side of the cabin and has four more soldiers following behind him.

As quickly as she stood up, she drops to the ground again. Not having any idea how many people are here right now, she realizes that she could never take them all on, and her dog follows her to the ground, trying to sniff his owner to see if she is OK. Closing her eyes, afraid they may have seen her, she tries to focus on her breathing and smells the scent of grass mixed with burnt wood. *I have to ride this pain out again.* Her breathing has started to calm down when she hears the vehicles start. The sound of the motors makes her squeeze her eyes tighter from the sudden noise; then she exhales, picking her head up from the grass to peek at them again, and sees the enemy driving down her dirt road and out of sight.

Turning her back to the burning cabin, she slides down the hill, leaning her back against it. Tears stream down her face from pure frustration while her place burns to the ground. She does not know how long she sat there, but she has no energy to move. Her muscles have tapped out for the day, and her head hurts from the emotions that have swept over her body. Feeling frozen in time, with tear streaks staining her face, she dazes off into some far-off dream where her son is playing at a playground, running around with other kids, and her husband is sitting on a bench with her, watching their child. Her husband's arm is around her, and they are both enjoying Linc's childhood, which is so happy and carefree—a distance memory of their life that was ripped away from them.

"Casey! Casey!" Jamie exclaims as she yanks her friend's shoulder back and forth trying to bring her back to reality. "Are you OK? What happened? Casey!"

"Mom, Mom!" Linc steps up next to his mother.

Looking into her son's eyes, all the anger sweeps through her again, and she grabs him, hugging him tightly.

"Yes, son, Mom is fine," she answers with a sharp tone.

Jamie decides to peek over the hill to investigate and freezes, seeing that where there had been a cabin yesterday, there is nothing but black and gray ashes now. Some of the ashes still glow with red and orange embers, but the fire is small and in control.

"Assholes!" Jamie says and sits down next to her friend.

"It is fine," Casey chokes out. "We are survivors and we will continue to prevail. Tomorrow I am going to teach you and Linc how to hunt; we need to learn how to maintain here. They are not coming back. We have water and shelter. As long as we can get food, we will survive," she says harshly in a cold monotone, feeling like a statue.

Turning to Linc, she places her hand on his head, then leans over for a side hug as he sits down between his mom and friend when she says, "We are always OK, son. We just keep pushing forward, fighting. That's all we can do."

Standing up, she walks back to the bunker to lie down and rest. Like an unemotional robot, she pushes each foot forward, moving through the motions. *We must keep going,* she keeps telling herself.

Chapter 14

For the next few months all three of them go out and practice shooting the bow, setting traps, and fishing. They study their survival books and learn how to decide what plant life is edible. Jamie and Linc become very good at hunting and tracking animals. Their canned foods last a lot longer because they use them as a side dish for their meat. Eating better than they have since this journey began makes them successful in their new life. The dogs are filling out again from the food, looking like the dogs Casey once knew, and their energy is up. Not having to walk every day, the group rebuilds their strength, and their minds are a lot sharper as their free time consists of playing board games and Casey's continuing to teach Linc how to read, write, and do math. Refusing to let go of the knowledge of the past, she wants it to be handed down to her son. If they are outside, they go down by the creek and play near the water. It is their decision on how to live and what to do with their time.

It is still considered winter, but the weather has been fairly warm. Casey thinks they are in late February as she attempts to keep track of the days in her notebook she found in the cabin. She feels it's important to write their history and explain what is happening to them, how they got to this point, and what they are doing to survive.

Excited for the summer to come, they plan to grow a garden and learn how to can and store food. When her husband started working on this bunker he bought an assortment of books on survival, hunting, gardening, and storing food. He believed that the knowledge in these books was important to study and read if they ever needed it.

Casey's son is stronger and more confident in the woods now. He knows the area well since this has become his new playground. He loves to practice shooting his bow and begs to shoot the guns, but Casey is not sure if he is old enough yet, though there is a BB gun that his dad put in the bunker, and Linc practices with it all the time. He has a good eye when aiming and can shoot small animals well. He is also skilled with a knife, not scared to skin and cook an animal. His big project now is learning about the different traps and where they are most useful. Every morning he checks on his traps and resets them, or comes home to decide what kind of trap he wants to try. It is amazing how adaptable her son has become.

They do not talk about the past because it hurts too much. With too many unanswered questions, they stop asking and just accept that this is the way life is now. Although Casey thinks about her husband, she has nothing positive to say. They are all processing the grief in their own way and push to survive, uncertain how long they can stay in the bunker and how long they will have peace. Until the group has to make a change Casey encourages Linc to learn as much as he can while they are not on the move, to make sure he can do everything on his own, just in case something happens to her or Jamie. It is her job now, as it was in her past life, to make sure her son can make it without his parents.

Early one morning Casey gets up with Komodo, who of course is her right-hand man for hunting, and they set out down by the stream to see what they can find. It is her turn to get up and hunt. Jamie and Linc go out together with Baby Girl one day, and then they switch the next day, and Casey goes out with Komodo, alternating days so everybody can rest and practice hunting. Some way down the creek she finds a spot that looks like a good place to post up and see what she can get today. She always likes being by the creek, listening to the trickling of the water and smelling the fresh dew in the morning mixed with the scent of the pine trees. Her dog lies in his usual spot right below the tree she's in. Casey gets comfortable sitting on a big branch high in the air.

She enjoys sitting in the tree for a few hours embracing the peace and quiet, but there isn't a deer in sight, but this is OK because the group has more food now than they ever had. As she snacks on some meat she adjusts her body in the tree to get more comfortable, when suddenly she hears some twigs breaking. The birds stop chirping, warning her that something is here, and they are ready to watch the show. Komodo picks up his head and twitches his ear to search for the sound while Casey grabs her bow that already has an arrow set in it, and she pulls back the draw string, ready to aim. She searches around the woods where she heard the sound, but she does not see anything.

"Can you help me, please? I am unarmed, and I really need some help." She hears a man's voice, though she cannot see him.

Casey points her arrow toward the sound of the voice, and her dog stands up and starts to growl in a low voice to warn any enemy in their midst. "Komodo, down," Casey states quietly as she continues to search the woods on the other side of the creek, sure that the voice is coming from over there. The dog lowers himself to the ground, continuing to growl quietly, complaining that she told him to stop.

"Come out and let me see you," she calls out into the forest as strongly and as confidently as she can.

A cold, numbing feeling sweeps over her as she looks around; survival of the fittest is kicking in, and she is ready to save her own life. He could have a gun or a knife. This voice may not belong to the only person out in the woods. Casey's panic mode is starting to take over while she tries to control her breathing.

"Please, truly I mean no harm. I am unarmed and starving. I escaped the camp and ran. Please, I am begging you," the man's voice pleads.

He is tricking me, I am sure of it! she thinks, before she says, "I need you to come out. I need to see you." Casey tries to sound strong, though she feels very vulnerable as he can see her but she cannot see him.

"OK… OK, please do not shoot me!" the voice calls out, sounding shaky and scared.

He steps out from behind a tree across the stream and slowly steps toward the creek. Casey points her arrow right for his chest now that she can see him and can size him up. Komodo gets up again and barks with his hair standing straight up as he warns this man to stay back. "Down, boy!" Casey commands again, trying to sound in control as she stares at this person, ready to shoot him.

Her dog sits down but never takes his eyes off the guy. He continues to growl in a low, mean voice. Casey keeps her bow in an attack position, ready to let go of the string, deciding if she should hear this man out. He is wearing a ragged shirt and jeans with holes where his knees are showing through. He is all skin and bones. Truly he looks like he is starving. His hair is a curly mess of grays and browns, and there is dirt all over his face and arms. His blue eyes are sunken into his head with dark shadows underneath them.

"Please, I beg, I won't hurt you, I promise. Do you have any food?" he asks, his voice shaking, and he puts up his hands to show he is not hiding anything.

She has a wrapped piece of meat that she was starting to eat. Quickly grabbing it, she throws it at him on the other side of the creek. Then she aims her bow back at him again. Watching him drop to his knees to grab at the food that fell at his feet, Casey stays silent while he devours it. After he is done he bends over and cups the water from the stream and takes a drink.

"You said you were at a camp. Where is that? What is it?" she asks, still keeping her bow pointing at him, deciding if she is going to trust this man.

He sits down in the grass and looks up at her with confusion and then smirks and looks down at the stream, shaking his head. Looking up at her again, he says, "Have you been out here in the woods this whole time?"

"No, I lived in town and ran before they caught me," she explains, narrowing her eyes, feeling angry that he is laughing at her.

"There is a camp outside of Keystone where people are enslaved. We are working in the mines trying to find gold. They are either working us to death, killing us, or shipping us off to only God knows where, because those people never come back. We are fed very little and forced to do hard physical labor," he explains without looking at her.

Lowering her bow, she looks in her bag and finds some more meat and throws it to him. The food falls next the man, and he grabs it, engulfing it as well. Her dog finally lies down, not feeling he is danger, though he is still watching the man closely, stretching out his nose, trying to sniff him from a distance.

Once the man is done eating he looks up at her again. "Thanks."

"How did you get out?" she asks.

He looks down again and says, "They were going to put me on the train. When I was outside of the fence waiting in line some men tried to fight to get free. During the commotion I slipped away and ran for the hills and never looked back."

"Was there a man who was six feet tall with black hair, a goatee, and dark eyes named Devon at the camp?"

"Lady, I have no idea. We were all packed in like cattle. There were way too many people, and by now he has probably been killed or sent away." With this, he laughs meanly and says, "You are better off staying out here than chasing ghosts." He then narrows his eyes and looks right at Casey. "You are lucky you did not get caught. The women are enslaved, killed, sent away, or worse, and I would not go back and chance it," he warns her.

Choking down her sadness, she leans back against the tree, absorbing everything this man just said. *What if he is still alive?* is all she can think. *I know he is a survivor. What if...*

"Are you by yourself?" the man asks, breaking her train of thought.

Looking down at him again, she wonders if she should tell him her story. "Yes, I am alone. And yes, I am going to that camp to find my husband."

"Ha! Good luck with that! You can count me out; I'm getting as far away as I can." He smirks at Casey and shakes his head. He stands up and starts walking away, knowing that this conversation is done.

"Wait. What direction is this camp?" she asks before he leaves.

He turns around, looking at her; then he points to the southeast and says, "It's a straight shot from here, but I am telling you, you are making a big mistake. People are slaves there, and you will be one of them."

"Here. Take this," she grabs her knife on her belt loop and throws it to him so he can attempt to hunt. Then she says, "What is your name?"

"Greg. Hey, thanks. And yours?" he asks, picking the knife off the ground to examine it.

"Casey. Till we see each other again…" she responds and nods her head.

The man lifts his chin back at her and walks off in the direction he came from. Casey waits until he is out of sight before she moves on, not wanting him to follow her back home. While she waits she thinks, *He must be really scared of the camp to not want to go with me. Leaving all by himself with nothing but a knife shows how horrible that place must be.* Once she feels it is safe, she climbs down from the tree. Komodo gets up and sniffs her to make sure she's OK. Casey pets him on the head for reassurance, and her dog wags his tail as they walk home, staying close as always and keeping an eye out for her.

Later that night after Linc falls asleep Casey tells her friend about the man she saw in the woods, explaining to her what he said about the camp and how everybody is enslaved.

"Why does anybody want to do that to us?" Jamie asks, confused and frustrated, narrowing her eyes as she tries to understand.

"Listen, Devon might be there," Casey says, trying to read what Jamie is thinking.

Jamie looks back and shakes her head, changing her facial expression from angry to concerned, seeing the hope in her friend's face. Then she says, "No… No, Casey, you do not know that he is. It is way too dangerous. Plus, what about Lincoln? He needs you here," she says, lifting her hands toward the sleeping child, worried about what Casey is saying.

"I just… just thought I would scout it out and maybe you and Linc could stay here. I want to see if he survived, if he is still alive," she explains, looking down at her feet, feeling her hope being crushed by reality.

"What if you don't return? What am I going to tell your son? This is stupid and not safe," Jamie says.

Still looking down, Casey says nothing, knowing she is right. *It is probably a terrible idea, but what if I could see him again?*

"You know we will be fine here, Linc and me. We know how to take care of ourselves; you taught us how to survive. But your son will be crushed if you don't come back," Jamie harshly spits out because she does not want to say this to her friend.

"I will come back," Casey says as intently as she can, looking back at Jamie and nodding her head. "I will be fast, and I will not do anything stupid," she says, quickly trying to talk her friend into this idea with new hope in her voice.

Jamie stares at her for a few minutes, looking deep into her eyes, trying to read her thoughts. Casey stares back at her friend's concerned blue eyes, trying to show confidence. Then Jamie sighs and says, "Fine, but you better come back!"

Smiling in relief, Casey jumps up and wraps her arms around her friend, saying, "Thank you. Oh, thank you. I will return, I will be safe, I promise!"

Lying down for bed that night, she thinks, *I may have a chance to see him. He could still be alive. Please, God, let him still be alive.*

The next morning she wakes up and prepares for her trip to Keystone. Finishing packing her bag, she decides to take Komodo with her so she is not alone. The trip will be faster with only herself and her dog to worry about. She figures Baby Girl will do better with the two she has been with since the start. Eventually Linc wakes up and watches his mom as she packs the last items needed for the trip.

"What are you doing?" he asks.

She stops and sits down next to her son. Turning to him, she looks into his face. His big brown eyes stare at her intently, waiting for an explanation. "Lincoln, I am going to go on a short trip. I will be gone for a few days and will return. I heard where some prisoners are being held and want to see if Daddy is there. You have to stay here to help Jamie hunt and take care of the place. Can you do this for me?" she asks, looking into her son's eyes to see what type of reaction she gets from him.

He glares at her and sharply says, "Are you coming back?"

"Yes, I am coming back, son. I always come back," she promises, giving him a big hug and whispering in his ear, "I love you, little buddy." Then she squeezes him tightly, and he squeezes her back, leaning his head on her chest and closing his eyes.

"Are you ready to go hunting?" Jamie asks Linc, standing near the door and listening the whole time.

"Bye, son. I will see you again," Casey says, seeing him look past her, lost in his own thoughts.

He then stands up, listening to Jamie with the saddest defeated look on his face. As Jamie puts her arm around his shoulder, she turns back to Casey with a weak smile, and they walk out together with Baby Girl following them.

Chapter 15

Once they are gone, Casey finishes packing her bag; then she straps Komodo's hiking pack to him, and they leave the bunker as well. Her dog stays next to her as they start their journey in the direction that Greg showed them. They move fast through the woods because she is more confident in her hunting skills, and she feels better knowing her son is in safe hands. Jamie and Linc have food, and they know how to hunt; plus, they have a shelter that is well hidden.

The weather has been gradually getting warmer with less snow. Though South Dakota's weather is unpredictable, it seems to be getting better. The sun is out heating up the cool morning, there are very few clouds in the sky, and a light breeze brushes against her face. The birds are out this morning singing their songs and flying around while Casey moves in a light jog through the forest. She has learned to step lighter to not scare the animals and to keep her ears on alert, listening to all the noises, feeling content in the woods as the Black Hills have become her home and way of life.

The days seem to blend together as she works her way closer to the town of Keystone. Thinking it has been over a week, Casey gets up for the morning and packs up in a hurry. She stops to kill and eat any animal she finds along the way and shares the food with her Pyrenees. She goes as far as she can every day, wanting to get to the camp and back to her son as soon as possible. Her child is her motivation to move quickly and keep one foot moving in front of the other, determined to keep her promise.

Finally, there is a big hill covered with pine trees she knows she needs to climb. Casey continues hiking up it for most of the day, and it sets her calves on fire. By late afternoon she makes it to the top where she sees the camp for the first time. The whole place is surrounded by a fence topped with barbed wire that abuts the bottom of the hill she is on, just like a prison. This place has to be over a hundred acres, and she can see a huge mine where people are working on the opposite side of the camp. To the east of the mine is a train track. *That is where Greg escaped*, she thinks as she sits down and continues to observe this place. Komodo follows his owner and finds a comfy spot with some grass next to her and circles around a few times before he lies down on his belly. On the outside of the fence line there are simple guard towers made out of wood with one soldier in each of them, pacing back and forth, watching everybody. Also, she can see men patrolling around the outside of the fence circling the prison. On the inside there are various buildings where people are coming and going for whatever tasks they are assigned.

Staring for a long time at this prison right here in the middle of the hills, only a week away from where they are living, makes her wonder how safe they are in the bunker. At the top of the hill she is well hidden in the trees, and she can see the camp clearly. People are moving around, but they are too far away for her to see their faces. Pulling off her bag, she searches around until she finds her binoculars and looks through them to scan everything more closely. Watching the guards shuffle people back and forth, she thinks that it is so sad to see so many people hurting. If prisoners do not comply, the soldiers hit or shoot them. Casey starts breathing deeply, trying to stay in control as she is overwhelmed by witnessing such a tragedy.

Clearly the men and women are in separate areas, with fences running down the middle of the camp. There is a canopy next to the middle fence on the women's side. On the men's side there is a huge carport-like shelter that meets the fence opposite the women's canopy. It almost looks like the two connect at the fence line. She cannot see underneath either roof, though she knows this area must be important since so many people keep coming from and going there.

The men and women seem to be late-teens or adults, but she sees no kids anywhere. *What happened to all the children?* she wonders as she keeps scanning the men, hoping to see her husband. Most of the people look the same: they all are starving, skin and bones with no weight in their faces or arms. All of them are dirty from head to toe. Some don't even have shoes, and while some have coats, most of them are wearing only t-shirts.

The men are being shuffled to and fro, going to the mine and coming back. Casey watches one guy fall to the ground, too tired to keep working, and everybody just keeps walking by until a guard brings a wheelbarrow and puts him in it and wheels him away from the crowd. Everybody else just keeps moving like this is nothing new, just another person who could not handle this terrible treatment anymore.

As she watches through her binoculars the poor man being removed, she finally sees him, or at least a worn-out version of her husband. "There he is," Casey says to Komodo, and she gets on her knees, stretching her body forward, trying to get closer. Her dog lifts his head and looks at his owner like he is listening, then goes back to licking his paw.

Devon is in a dirty white t-shirt and black dress pants. They are the clothes he was wearing the day they were attacked. *He has been in his dress clothes this whole time and must be cold with such a thin layer of garments on.* He is so thin, and looking at his body, she can see that his cheek bones and eye sockets are sunk in his face. She watches him turn his head and glare at the guards who are walking by with the guy in the wheelbarrow. *Thank God, it looks like his spirit is still strong. He hasn't given up yet,* she thinks. She stares at him as he joins the line walking under the huge canopy. She waits, watching the building for a while, afraid she may lose her husband now that she cannot see him anymore. After a while he comes out, and Casey keeps her eyes on him as he walks around the camp to the side of the fence line closest to her. He sits down, leaning against the fence, and a couple of men join him, and they stay there for hours into the night. Finally, a guard comes by, and they all get up. Devon leaves the other two and goes into what looks like an oversized, beat-up trailer.

Putting down her binoculars, she gets up and goes to the other side of the hill, finding a hidden spot, and sets up her tent. Lying down for the night, Casey pets her dog, who leans against her as he lies down. They stay in that position for what seems like forever while tears stream from her eyes as she thinks about her husband being alive and treated like a slave. *If I could only find a way to sneak him out of there. I will watch for a few days and see if there is a weak spot somewhere that I can use to my advantage.* After many hours of staring into the darkness, her eyes are too heavy to keep open and her brain shuts down for the night.

For the next few days Komodo and Casey sit and scout the camp. She watches the morning shift of guards and how they treat the prisoners. They are eager to hit or shoot the people if they do not comply. Devon minds these watchmen, although she saw him clenching his fists a few times, trying to hold back from hitting them as they yell in the prisoners' faces.

The soldiers in the mine are probably the worst of them. They are quick to shoot anyone who does not work. Watching them mine, Casey can see a dirt road that circles into the deep hole. Only parts of the mine are visible from her location, so she cannot see how deep it really is, but she notices the wheelbarrows placed along this road, waiting for someone to fall over or be shot. A ledge has been dug out right above the road, and the slaves are standing on it, chipping away the sides of the mountain. If someone tries to fight back, they are killed. Other prisoners stand by the wheelbarrows, waiting to get the bodies of the guys who give up. She never sees anybody with food or water and does not think they are being fed, even though Greg said that they were given a small amount of food. The guards on the outside of the fence march along and pass by Casey's side of the camp every thirty minutes or so, walking in pairs as they circle the prison. She sees different sets of soldiers walk in front of her as if this is all they do each day. None of them seem too worried about the prisoners' leaving, nor do they watch in the woods to see if anybody is hiding in them, instead always talking in deep conversations and apparently bored with their daily task.

The evening watchmen are a little calmer. If someone falls over, the other prisoners are able to grab them and put them in the trailer. As long as they don't fight back, these guards show a small amount of kindness and mercy, allowing the prisoners to move a little more freely by the sleeping units that seem to be designated for the prisoners. Watching the people fill the trailers at night, it looks like too many people are assigned to each unit. She counts over thirty people step into one of the double-wides and thinks, *How do the people have any room to sleep?*

The late-night-to-early-morning guards are the most laid back of them all. Very few soldiers are seen moving around in the camp, and it looks like the tower watchmen keep an eye on the prisoners in the late hours of the night. The tower guard that is closest to Casey, where Devon likes to sit by the fence line, seems to sleep on his shift, not really watching anybody. Finally, the last shift change of the closest watchman, somewhere in the wee hours of the morning, seems to be the weakest of them all. Gazing at him closely, she sees he does the same thing every night: he gets up in the tower, sits down, and drinks. He likes to drink a lot, and she is sure it is alcohol. After about an hour she sees him lean his head against the rail, and he falls asleep or passes out. This soldier is the only thing between Casey and getting her husband out of the prison. She does not see any other guards walk the fence line at night, which will make it easier to get closer to Devon.

Most of the prisoners in this wee hour are trying to sleep. They are too tired to sneak out and find the weak spots. If she could only find a way to get her husband's attention to let him know she is here, if he would get up in the early hours, Casey might have a chance to save him. She sees that some prisoners do wander that late at night on the grounds, but they do not give anybody problems, and the guards do not mess with them. *How can I get to him through the fence and send a message?*

she ponders. *I see people leaning against the chain link, so I know it is not electrical. Maybe I can get down close without getting caught.*

The next day Casey packs up and hikes around the back side of the mountain with her trusty companion by her side to see if they can find a cabin that may have some tools or something that can help them. She spends most of the morning wandering around until she comes across a few spots where homes have been burnt to the ground. Looking through the ashes of each place they come across, she hopes something has survived, any item she can use. At one of the houses, she pushes the ashes around and finds a human skull lying in the pile. Jumping back, Casey panics, realizing it is a dead person, while Komodo walks into the ashes, right to the human bones, and sniffs them. *Were they killed before the fire or during the fire?* Casey thinks, and she steps back to the ashes, pushing them around with a stick, searching, determined to find what she needs to save her husband and reunite her son with his dad.

"Come on, Komodo. We cannot help them," she finally says, not seeing anything she can use, and steps away. The deaths do not affect her the way they used to; she is becoming numb to the tragedy that she sees daily. Before, she could barely keep her stomach under control; now, she looks at them and just moves on, knowing she cannot do anything.

Well into the afternoon Casey finally comes across a little cabin that has been ignored. She stares at it for a while, hidden in the trees, to see if there is any activity in it. The cabin standing in front of her is still and silent. On front porch sit two rocking chairs, with a shed to the side of the cabin. She waits and thinks that maybe they just missed this place or that they didn't burn every home. After a while, she steps toward the shed, her pistol out, ready to shoot, in case somebody appears. Casey gets to the shed, opens it, and looks inside to see that it is a small workshop. Komodo pokes his head inside, though there is not enough room for him to enter. Tools are neatly displayed on a bench against the back wall. It is well organized, which makes her think somebody cares for this shop.

Rummaging around in the drawers, she finds wire cutters and a note-book, which is small enough to put in a man's shirt pocket. Next to it are some pens. Grabbing the items, she packs them in her bag. Thinking she could use a flashlight and batteries at their bunker, she grabs them and connects the light to a clip hanging on the outside of her bag.

Then Casey steps out of the shed and shuts the door, hiding the fact that she ever disturbed it. Walking around to the front of the cabin, she peeks into the windows to see that it is deserted. *Probably, this is a summer cabin and this person was caught in town.* Stepping up to the door, she tries to open it, but it doesn't budge. Looking down at the porch, Casey sees a flower pot with a dead flower in it. Thankfully there is a key sitting under it, and she is able to unlock the door and slowly goes inside. With her pistol out, she takes a step into the living room and looks around. The silence engulfs her, and with every step she can hear the creak of the wooden floor. Walking to the kitchen, she checks the pantry for food and finds canned veggies and fruit. Loading up her bag and Komodo's pack with what she can, she searches through the drawers and finds a fork. Once Casey is satisfied she leaves behind what she cannot carry. Stepping out of the cabin, she locks the door, places the key back under the flower pot, and heads back to camp, thinking about how to get her husband's attention. Her loyal dog and friend is by her side every step of the way.

"Come on, boy. Let's get Dad," she says as they make their way back to the prison.

Chapter 16

Once they are back in their scouting spot overlooking the slave camp, Casey sits down and uses her pocket knife to open a can of beans and placing them in Komodo's collapsible bowl; then she opens peaches for herself. Her dog lies down with his head in the bowl, enjoying a nice treat, while his owner watches the prison and eats as well. She thinks about when the best time to get Devon's attention will be and contemplates what she is going to do for the rest of the day. *I will have to get closer to get a message to him.*

"How are we going to get Dad's attention?" she asks Komodo. He nudges her hand with his nose, and she pets his head as he army-crawls closer to his owner, and she smiles, enjoying the comfort. Seeing that the sun is starting to go down and the weather is getting cooler, she decides to go to bed early tonight, hoping things will work out tomorrow. Placing the dog's bowl back in his bag, they go back to the other side of the hill. Lying down for the night, she whispers a prayer: "Jesus, please bless us tomorrow, protect us, and help us get Devon's attention. In Jesus's name… Amen." She wraps her arm around her dog lying close by her, and she listens to him sigh before she drifts off to sleep.

The next morning, before the sun is out, Casey wakes up feeling groggy from a lack of sleep, as her mind raced all night. She steps out of the tent and Komodo follows her. They both walk down the mountain to get closer to the fence line of the camp. Moving slowly and quietly and trying not to disturb the noise of the woods, Casey finds a big mess of tangled-up branches to hide behind about thirty feet away from the fence. Sitting down in the dirt, she pulls out the small notebook and writes, "Here early morning hours." Then she pokes a hole through the paper and attaches it to an arrow. Finally, she readies her bow and places it on the ground against a tree trunk.

"Komodo, down," Casey quietly instructs her dog, pointing at the dirt. He lies down, sighing in frustration as his owner pats his head to calm him. They sit in this place for hours watching the camp. People are shifting around throughout the day, and she watches as some slaves sit against the fence and others stand talking. The soldiers walk by the fence, continually chatting amongst themselves. Taking a deep breath, she braces herself every time they patrol by, worried they may look in her direction; but the guards don't notice her or her animal and continue their daily business, talking with each other, not seeing anything that is messing with their rhythm of life. After the watchmen pass Casey releases her breath, glad they didn't notice or have a reason to look in their direction. Being only thirty feet away from the camp, she worries they are going to get caught.

By midafternoon Casey is getting pretty anxious. She knows Devon will be sitting in front of her very soon. Shifting back and forth, trying to stretch her legs and get ready to signal him, she hopes that he follows the same pattern he has been following since she found the camp. She keeps an eye on the guard in the tower, who is standing over and watching the camp. He looks around intensely trying to find someone doing something wrong. He paces from one end of the tower, looking where Devon normally sits, back in the other direction, holding his rifle ready to react to anyone who disobeys. Casey watches his movement continually to make sure she knows where he is.

Finally, she sees her husband. He is so close, which makes her want to get up and run to him. It takes everything she has to hold back her urges. Walking over to his spot, he moves slowly, and she can see how tired he is. Devon looks sad and defeated. *I hate seeing him in such a devas-*

tating state, she thinks. Now she can clearly see how skinny he is. *I am sure he is cold with only a t-shirt and dress slacks on.* He sits down, leaning against the fence that is standing between them. Then two men sit down next to him. Casey can see they are Devon's family. One is Connor, his younger brother, and the other is Steve, his dad.

Connor, only a couple of years younger than Devon, is about six feet tall and very skinny. He used to work out all the time, but the camp has broken down his muscles. He has black wavy hair and bright blue eyes. With a slight smile and a twinkle in his eyes, he could always get a girl's attention. He knew he could, too. With his over-confidence and ego, he was always carefree and enjoyed life. Looking at him now, it breaks Casey's heart to see no smiles, no twinkle in his eyes. He is worn out and looks so ragged and cold, with little clothing, like Devon.

As for Steve, he was a slightly heavier man with short hair that has highlights of grey coming in. He has always been a jolly man, ready to joke around and have fun. He worked hard for his family but loved to kick back and enjoy his time. Family has always meant more to him than anything else. Now he is noticeably a lot thinner, and he is also under-dressed, wearing only a t-shirt with torn blue-jeans and no coat. It is so hard to sit out here, free, and see the people she knows and loves hurting the way that they are.

Another set of guards walk by the fence between Casey and her husband, which brings her train of thought back to the task at hand. Holding her breath, she watches them pass by. Once they are gone she picks up her bow that is set to shoot. She aims it at the ground right between Devon and his dad, hoping she can get the arrow close enough for them to notice without hitting them. She keeps her bow steady as she looks at the tower to make sure the guard is looking the other direction. The watchman glances at her husband and then turns his back and takes a few steps to the other end of the tower to check out the other side of the camp. Looking again at her husband, she checks her aim one last time. "Please, Jesus," she says, her heart racing as she releases the arrow. It flies through the air and hits the ground, sliding in the dirt through one of the holes of the chain-link fence. Lowering her body to hide again, Casey stares at Devon to see what he does next. He jumps in his sitting position, startled by the arrow that just hit between him and his dad. The very end of the arrow sticks out of the ground with the small folded paper attached to it. He turns his back and looks in her direction. "Please see me, please see me," she whispers out loud, still hidden. Komodo's ears stand up, and he turns his head to the side, wondering what she is doing.

Devon places his hand over the paper and feathers, turning his back to his wife, and faces forward again. Steve nudges him, and they both look up to see the tower guard now pacing back and looking over toward them. Her husband keeps his hand over the arrow, still acting like nothing is going on, as normal as can be. All three of them look stiff and uncomfortable. Casey watches as another set of guards come near the fence line again, and she sees the boys all take a deep breath, staying still and silent to see what is going to happen next. Quietly Casey starts to pet Komodo's head while staring, too.

After a few seconds the watchman in the tower paces back in the other direction again, and the patrolling guards walk by, lost in their own conversation. Once nobody is watching Devon grabs the paper and pushes the arrow deeper into the ground to hide it. He looks at the paper, and then he looks up, handing it over to Connor, who reads it and hands it to his dad. The boys sit still for a few minutes, not doing anything; then they all stand up nonchalantly and turn toward Casey. She grabs the flashlight hanging from her bag and glances at the tower guard, who is still looking in the other direction, and she takes a chance to flash the light on and off.

Devon looks at the blinking flash and raises his eyebrows as he makes eye contact with his wife. She stops breathing as her heart starts racing when she sees him looking at her. She leans forward and grabs a branch in front of her, lowering it a little, then watches Steve grab his son's arm to break their gaze. Devon looks at his dad, and they all look away from the fence, walking separate ways. She stares at her husband as he walks into his trailer and disappears. Letting out a deep breath, she whispers, "He saw us, Komodo. He saw us."

Casey stays in her spot, hidden behind the tangled branches, well into the evening, waiting until it is dark enough to retreat back to the top of the hill and out of danger. She is not willing to take any more chances today. Once it is safe they sneak quietly back up the hill to sit, wait, and watch the camp, wanting to see if Devon comes out in the early morning hours. *If he does, what will the guards do?*

Komodo and Casey rest for most of the night, waiting for the shift change of the tower watchmen. The more she thinks about getting Devon out, the more anxious she gets. Her feelings bounce from being nervous to see if the boys will come out and how the guards will react, to excitement, thinking about getting her husband back to his son. She wants to be the hero for her son, knowing she cannot save everyone here, but maybe she can at least save Devon. Finally, in the wee hours of the morning, Casey sees her husband, Connor, and Steve come out of their trailers and sit down in the same spot as they had earlier in the day. The tower guard notices them sit down, and he slows down his drinking, watching the boys suspiciously for a good hour or two before the guys get up and go back to their trailers to sleep.

As they walk back to their separate trailers Casey hopes they come back tomorrow. She and her dog retreat back to their tent and go to sleep. The next few nights she watches the boys come out, waiting for something to happen, though nothing ever does. She keeps an eye on the guard, who cares less and less about them with each passing night. By the fourth night the guard is back to his usual habit of drinking until he passes out.

Early in the morning on the fifth day, Casey sees dark clouds rolling in; the temperature is dropping fast and the wind is picking up. She knows a storm is settling in and decides that today is the day. Today is the day that she will attempt to get her husband out, so she packs up everything since this is the last night she will stay here. She and Komodo make their way down the hill in the early-morning hours. The snow starts to fall by late morning, and they make their way to her spot in the tree line, hiding behind the clump of branches, Komodo by her side. She and her dog get comfortable, sitting on the snowy dirt to wait. The snow continues to fall throughout the day, and the wind continues to blow harder and harder. Hunkering down, trying to cuddle up with her Pyrenees for warmth, she waits for her moment. By late afternoon there is already a foot of snow covering the ground, and it continues to build up around them. The wind howls, causing the snow to blow around everywhere. By nightfall the visibility is terrible. She can barely see the fence line from this position, and she keeps thinking that the worse the weather gets, the better it will be for them.

Komodo is enjoying the snow that is building up around him. He continues to nudge his nose into it and eats it. Casey has to keep telling him to sit down because he just wants to play. His coat is made for this weather, and she watches the puppy-like attitude spilling out of him. Every time she gets on to him he lies down and sighs in frustrations. She smiles, seeing him enjoy this freezing weather.

The camp never slows down. The guards push the prisoners into the mines as if there were no blizzard. Most of them do not have the right clothes for this weather, including her husband. Casey is layered and well insulted in her garments, yet she can still feel the cold biting at her. Waiting for the time to pass, she focuses on her breath of white clouds, trying to make rings over and over again, thinking her only hope is that her husband will push through knowing somebody out here is trying to help him. She watches many of the people fall as conditions are too harsh to want to continue; it's so easy to just give up. It is difficult to watch, knowing she cannot save them. She cannot free them all, and they are dying due to the mistreatment by these evil people.

Casey tries over and over to make breath rings just to pass the time, while Komodo moves back and forth. He is ready to get up and stretch, tired of sitting in the same spot. Every time he tries to move Casey tells him to sit back down. He glares at her in frustration and lies down with his head away from his owner to show his disapproval. Petting his back, she tries to let him know that she understands his frustration, but he huffs and puffs at his owner, ignoring her pets.

By the time it is close to midnight the visibility is incredibly poor. She can barely see the wires of the chain-link fence. The bottom of the tower is still visible and piled up with snow, while the top is blurry, lost in the winter wonderland. The wind continues to howl fiercely, not ready to give in, and Casey continues to rock back and forth to keep herself warm. *Please show up, please show up*, she thinks, trying to ignore the pain from the wind whipping snow in her face. Finally, the change in guard comes, and Casey gets on her knees, stretching out, knowing that this is the hour they have been waiting for. Komodo sits up, watching also. She pets her dog as she stares intensely at the guard, trying to see what he is doing, though it is hard to tell. Barely able to see him, Casey grabs her binoculars and stares at the watchman, who sharply sits down, looking unhappy with the weather, and starts to swig at his bottle to warm his veins. Eventually he leans his head back on a post with his eyes closed.

Then she sees Devon with his arms crossed, rubbing himself trying to keep warm. He looks out in her direction and then sits down. Next she watches Steven and Connor meet up with her husband, sitting down next to him. They are all shivering trying to stay warm, rocking back and forth, while Casey keeps an eye on the guard, who doesn't budge from his spot, ignoring his job completely. Looking back at the boys, she can barely see them, but she knows it is them. They work all day in this freezing weather, and now they are waiting, hoping to be set free.

It's time. All or nothing—that is where we are. All conditions are right to save them, she thinks. Komodo is ready to move, antsy from sitting all day. He stretches his back legs, dipping his head toward the snow, and arches his back; then he pulls up, stretching his front legs and sticking his nose in the air. Casey grabs his harness and attaches the wire clippers to it. She hugs him, and he whines a little while pushing his head into her chest.

"I know, buddy," she says, hugging her dog, who seems to know it is his turn to be the hero. She continues to watch while petting the dog, trying to give him some comfort. It looks like the main guard is sleeping, lost in a drunken stupor, and she cannot see the other guard towers due to the weather, so hopefully they cannot see her either. "Alright, boy, go to Daddy. Go, boy, get Dad," she says, swatting Komodo's back.

He steps out from behind the branches. His white fur blends in well in the blizzard conditions, and he is barely visible. He peers around, bending his knees, checking for people, unsure if he wants to keep going. Then slowly he takes one step at a time toward Devon. Once he is about ten feet from the fence, he looks up at the tower and then lowers his body to the ground. He crawls the rest of the way.

Devon turns his head to the fence to see Komodo crouched down, trying to sniff him through the links. Once he smells his owner, a familiar smell, he starts to stand back up.

"Down, boy," his owner whispers to his dog and gestures for him to lie down. Devon looks up to see if the guard has noticed the dog, but the watchman continues to sit in his chair with his eyes closed and his hands clenching his bottle. He snores loudly, and Devon can see his mouth opening and closing with the snoring motions, the guard unaware of what is going on right below him.

Komodo turns his body to show the wire clipper, and Devon puts his hand through the chain-link fence to unstrap the tool. Once the tool is untied his dog jumps back and dashes in Casey's direction. She stands on her feet ready to run if her dog is seen. Her hands are holding her pistol ready to aim and shoot, her eyes on the watchman as she tensely stares at what is going on. Komodo races back to her and lies low in the snow behind his owner, trying to hide, sensing how dangerous this is for him. He does not want to be anywhere near that prison, and she can't blame him. Everybody freezes for a few seconds to see if anybody just saw this big dog dodge its way back into the woods. After a few minutes of silence, Casey bends down behind the bushes, still on her feet, ready to run. One hand lets go of the gun, and she pets her dog to comfort him. "Good boy, Komodo," she whispers, watching her husband.

Connor and Steve look around, checking for the guards, while Devon slowly takes the clippers and cuts into the links of the fence. After the first cut they all stop and look around. Nobody notices, so her husband continues cutting, moving faster while his hands shake from the cold or maybe from fear; either way, she can see how hard it is for him to concentrate. He continues to cut, again and again, until the hole is big enough for him to get out.

Casey believes at this point that the main guard is fully passed out; he has not moved an inch since the breakout began. Casey stands up, wondering if she needs to get closer to her husband in case he needs help. Devon, still nervous, looks up to see if the watchman has moved. Once he is confident he slips through the cut fence and uses all his strength to hold it open for his brother and father. Once all three of them are out they scurry quietly in the direction Komodo ran. Casey is on her toes watching her husband go from scurrying into a full-fledged run to the woods once he sees her. Frozen in disbelief that he is here with her after all these months, she starts breathing hard from excitement, thinking, *Lincoln is going to have his Dad back.*

Devon is in a full sprint and runs right to Casey and picks her up easily, hugging her and swinging around in a circle. Embracing his hug that consumes her after going so many months without it, thinking he would never hug her again, she melts in his arms. He sets her down, gently cupping her face with his hands. He pulls his wife into his passion and kisses her. Giving into him, she is eager for his comfort and love.

"Come on! We have to leave, or they will catch us," Connor says harshly as he catches up to his brother.

Pulling back, Casey looks at them and see them shaking from the freezing weather. She has to get them somewhere safe, and fast. They all look at her for an answer on what to do now. "OK, hmmm… I know there is a cabin not too far from here that we can go to," she says, turning and leading the boys up the hill. *They are not safe yet. Connor is right: we have to keep going*, she thinks. Running at a light jog, they race up the hill in the direction of the cabin. If they can move fast enough, maybe they will be gone before the guards realize people have escaped.

Chapter 17

After jogging around this hill for a couple of hours in the thick snow with very little visibility, they finally make it to the abandoned cabin where Casey originally found the tools. Stepping ahead of the boys, she moves the flower pot and grabs the key, unlocks the door, and steps in first, and the group follows. Once everybody is in she shuts the door, and they stop to breathe for a second. Shaking his fur coat to get the wet snow off, Komodo lies down on the rug near the door to rest.

"Thank you, thank you, Casey," Steve says and hugs her.

Then Connor follows suit, embracing his sister-in-law. "I am forever grateful. Thank you so much."

"It's fine," she says to her brother-in-law. "I think there are bedrooms in the back." She nods her head toward the hall. "You guys need to find some clothes and bags. There is canned food in the kitchen. We need to grab what we can and leave."

As the boys go to the back rooms to see what they can find, Casey heads into the kitchen, grabbing another can of peaches. She passes by the kitchen table and puts down her pistol, then opens the pantry door as Devon steps up behind her. Closing her eyes, she takes a deep breath to savor the time she missed with her husband. He gently tilts his head down while placing his hands on her hips, and she can feel the heat of his breath and the movement of his lips near her skin. "My hero," he whispers seductively and gently kisses her neck. She feels a surge of electricity running through her veins. Casey smiles weakly as she gives into her husband's gentleness.

"Hey, lovebirds, I am going to check outside to see if the weather is clearing up," Steve says as he peeks into the kitchen.

Opening her eyes, she looks at her father-in-law with content and thinks, *We are all going to be OK.* Devon's father smiles and steps outside as Connor shoves his way into the small kitchen. "I am so hungry," he states, reaching around them to get to the canned food and placing it into a bag he found. Casey steps out of the way to let him get what he needs. Devon smiles at his wife as he grabs a can of fruit and sits down at the table to eat. She joins her husband at the table, glad to see that both boys found layers of clothes and boots to wear. Her brother-in-law fills his bag with food, and once he steps out Devon gets up and stuffs his bag as well. Taking over his brother's seat, Connor sits at the table and starts to eat.

Just as he finishes his food they all hear gunshots outside. The group stops what they're doing and look at each other. Her husband rushes out of the kitchen, being the first one to react, and grabs the gun his wife left on the table and moving swiftly into the living room. Connor jumps up from the table and follows right behind his brother. Lastly Casey follows, pulling out another pistol from inside her coat pocket. As her husband enters the living room the cabin door opens, and two soldiers burst inside, staring at them. They raise their guns, but Devon moves quicker with his pistol already in the air and aims and shoots one in the chest. At the same time Komodo jumps up and bites the other solider in the arm, pulling his gun down, which goes off as it hits the floor. The second solider falls to the ground, trying to fight off Komodo, as Devon turns his gun to this man with all his built-up anger, and with no mercy, he shoots him in the head. His brother pushes past everybody, running outside, into the blizzard. Peering through the falling snow, Casey can see Steve lying on the ground with blood pooling around him. She runs out of the house behind her brother-in-law and can see the bullet wound in his chest. She drops next to him, placing both of her hands on his wound, trying to stop the bleeding. Her dog follows behind, circling Steve and sniffing his body, trying to understand what is happening. The snow whips around, but everybody is too upset to feel the weather as snowflakes sticks to their faces.

"No! No!" she cries, shaking her head, with tears falling from her face. "You have to live. No! Please!"

Steve grabs his son's hand as he starts to cough up blood. Devon steps over his wife as his dad turns and looks at his little brother. They watch him attempt to smile at his boy while suffering from the pain. Then he turns his head, focusing on Casey, and says while coughing, "Save… save my boys. Get them out of here."

Devon grabs his wife's shoulders and states, "Come on. We have to go. Connor, let's go!"

"It's Dad!" his little brother yells.

"Go, son, go," their father says with all his might while he coughs again. They all watch his head sway toward his younger son, and he stops breathing.

"No!" Connor cries.

It is my fault, Casey thinks as she starts to hyperventilate, losing control of the situation. *If I had only left them alone... If I had insisted that we keep going, he would still be alive.*

Methodically she raises her hand over Steve and closes his eyes. Komodo licks Steve's arm while whining as Casey stands up slowly, trying to control herself, and quietly steps away from her father-in-law. With one heavy step at a time, she walks away from the man she has known for the last ten years of her life. He was Lincoln's grandpa and was there for his first steps and first baseball game, but now he's gone. They have no time to bury him or do anything, knowing that more soldiers are coming. It is only a matter of time before they will be up here. *We must leave. Linc needs his parents,* she thinks as she moves faster.

Rushing back into the house, she grabs their bags and comes back out to see Connor losing control as he lies over his Dad and her husband trying to pull his brother up. Finally standing up, he glares at Devon for not showing any emotion. He jerks his arm away from his brother and, with full force, closes his fist and hits her husband in the face. Komodo starts barking at Connor, stepping between the boys, trying to break up the fight, while her husband staggers backward, trying to hold his composure, and almost falls over. He looks at his little brother, surprised that he turned all his anger at him, and says, "Connor, we have to leave, or they are going to kill us. Please, just come with us."

Her husband has turned off all his emotions, and Casey can see the dullness in his eyes as he tries to help his little brother. As if a switch has been flipped, he becomes a statue in motion, trying to push his brother forward. Then he sticks his hand out to his brother. "Come on. You are all I have left. Please—we have to go now."

Finally, his little brother breathes in deeply and slowly reaches for one of the bags from his sister-in-law, puts it on, and walks away from his father. Devon reaches for the other pack; then the group slowly walks away from the cabin with Komodo following. Once they get in the rhythm of walking Casey looks down at her hands to see Steve's blood all over them; then she speeds up until she is in a full run. Sprinting away from the horror of what just happened, racing away from everything and everyone, is all she can do and control. Komodo stays right at her heels, unwilling to leave his owner's side. Devon and Connor try to follow, but they are too weak to run as fast, and they lose her. Eventually running out of breath, she slows down but continues to walk fast while she tries to catch her breath and allows the boys to catch up.

"Casey!" Devon yells to his wife. "Casey!" Saying nothing back, she keeps moving and thinks, *What can I say to him? Sorry your dad died while we were eating, kissing, and hanging out? I knew better. We should have left right away! That is how I survived so long: by going without stopping.* "They are coming for us; let's just keep moving."

They spend the next week walking through the hills, not saying much to each other. Because of all the canned food they took from the cabin, they do not need to hunt. Devon and Connor have more food in their bags than they have had in months. The group moves as fast as they can through the forest, afraid that soldiers may be following them. Much of the time Casey is lost in her own thoughts, ignoring the boys. Her mind races, thinking about the problems of her life, how every time she gets what she wants she loses something or someone for it, and she wonders if it is all worth the heartache. In the late afternoon on the fifth day they stop to take a break by a creek and get a drink of water. Connor steps away from the group, giving Casey and Devon some privacy to talk.

"What happened to you?" Casey finally builds up the courage to ask.

He takes a drink of water and then stares at the creek, watching the water rush away from them, before he says, "I was at work in my office, staring at the computers, when the electricity went out. My co-workers and I joked around for a while, thinking the power would come back on, but it didn't. I tried to use my cell phone, and it would not work either. Finally giving up, I started to walk to the truck when the military guys showed up. They all had guns and threatened we go with them or they would shoot us. A bunch of my co-workers tried to overpower them, but it did not work, and they died. Since I was further away, I watched them shoot and kill my friends. I didn't have my guns, so I cooperated, just trying to survive. At the camp I found my brother and dad, but I could not find you. I saw that there were no kids, so I was not sure if you got caught or if you were dead. They made us slaves working in the mines, and we barely ate anything. It was only a matter of time before we were going to die. People just cannot live in those kinds of conditions."

For a few seconds Casey thinks about what Devon said; then she responds, "Who are they? Who are the bad guys?"

"I don't really know. They did not talk to us or help us. In fact, if they showed any act of kindness to the prisoners, they were punished too. I don't really understand what this is all about."

As they make their way through the hills the weather starts to warm up and the storm goes away. It is like God dumped the snow on them just to sneak Devon out. Every day on the way back to the bunker the sun comes out, finally melting the snow away as the temperature warms up. The wind blew away the clouds and now has calmed down, leaving behind a blue sky. Casey can hear the birds chirping and the streams trickling. The trip through the woods is fast with the boys, who want to do nothing but get to their destination so they can rest. Komodo enjoys moving through the woods with his other owner back. Every time they stop for a break he jumps up and down on Devon, wanting all of his attention.

Finally, late in the afternoon and after a little over a week, the sun is starting to set above the hill that they are walking up. The rays stretch across the hill top, over the dry grass. Casey can see the stream that is behind their property in front of them, where this journey began, where she met Greg, who told her about the camp. She stops and takes a deep breath of fresh air as her husband looks on, wondering what she is doing. Connor follows his brother's lead, and they both stare at her weirdly. Komodo stops to take a drink while wagging his tail, knowing this area. Casey gives a weak smile and says, "We're here."

The boys both turn around and look up at the top of the hill, toward the orange and yellow rays from the bright sun that is starting to set. The streams of light create an outline of a figure at the top of the hill. Casey shields her eyes from the rays, squinting to see better. The dark figure is Lincoln. He has his bow up, pointing at a tree on top of the hill. He does not notice the group and places another arrow in his bow, pulls back the string, and lets go. They all watch it fly through the air and hit the middle of the tree.

Looking over at Devon, Casey sees tears welling up in his eyes. He watches his son intensely; then he yells with all his might: "Linc! Lincoln!"

His son turns and looks toward them and narrows his eyes, squinting, trying to see who they are. Then he stammers out loud, "Da-Dad!"

Devon runs in a full sprint toward his son while Linc drops his bow and races down the hill to his dad. They meet in the middle, and her husband grabs his son and lifts him up. He holds onto his child for dear life, hugging his kid. His son closes his eyes, embracing his father. Then Devon lifts him high above his head as he circles around, smiling. They dance in the sun's rays, and for just a moment everything is as good as it is going to get. Tears stream from Casey's eyes as she pulls away from watching such a beautiful moment and looks past them. At the top of the hill leaning against a tree is her friend Jamie, who is smiling and nodding her head at Casey, knowing that she kept her promise. Smiling back, she looks down, watching as Komodo sits next to her with his tongue out, grinning from ear to ear. She pets his head as Baby Girl runs down the hill to greet them. Casey turns back to her husband and son. Seeing her child crying with tears of happiness, she can finally say that she got Lincoln's dad back. She has no idea what the future has in store for their family, but at least they are together again.

Epilogue

Even though Casey survived the first attack and she found a way to bring her husband and son back together, she still worries for the future. She knows the enemy is taking over her town and enslaving the people. Darkness looms around her family as they continue to survive in the woods. Linc is growing up in a life of violence and must be taught how to protect himself. With a camp full of prisoners not far away from their hideout, Casey knows that she will see the enemy again. As the family grows stronger, the war will rage on. The unclear reason for the attack hangs over her head, as she will have to decide if they are going to fight or hide. Only the future holds her fate as they enter the next chapter of their lives. With so many questions unanswered, she knows in her heart that this is only the beginning.

Acknowledgements

I would like to express my great appreciation to Indigo River Publishing for publishing my book.

Within the Indigo teams, I would like to give a special thanks to Bobby Dunaway, my production manager; Robin Vuchnich for the cover design and internal layout; Jay McCall, the lead marketer; and Earl Tillinghast, my editor. Without these teams, this book would not be possible. Thank you for all of your hard work on my project.